Vampir

BLOOD REUNION

...a flash of light caught her eye. Glancing toward the living room, she saw that something shiny and metallic lay on the floor. She picked her way carefully through the hall, past the sodden skeleton of what had once been the couch. All at once she gasped. A glittering golden chalice was half-buried in the ashes. She recognized it at once – it was from Aunt Gabrielle's hidden treasure.

The thief must have dropped this one cup. Ari picked it off the floor and rubbed it against her jeans legs, then tilted it to let the moonlight dance on its smooth, oval jewels. A vague dread seized her. Vampire gold...

NIGHTMARES

Vampire Twins 4

BLOOD REUNION

Janice Harrell

HarperCollins*Publishers*

First published in the USA in 1995 by
HarperCollins Publishers, Inc.
First published in Great Britain in 1995

1 3 5 7 9 10 8 6 4 2

Lions is an imprint of HarperCollins Children's Books,
a division of HarperCollins*Publishers* Ltd, 77-85 Fulham
Palace Road, Hammersmith, London W6 8JB

ISBN 0 00 675138 5
The author asserts the moral right to be identified
as the author of the work.

Produced by Daniel Weiss Associates, Inc.,
33 West 17thStreet, New York, New York 10011
Printed and bound in Great Britain
by HarperCollins Manufacturing Ltd, Glasgow

CHAPTER ONE

A SINGLE LAMP BURNED IN THE BACK OF THE JAGUAR dealership, where the fat salesman sat at his desk. "We don't usually stay open this late," he said nervously, "but anything to oblige a customer. Do you . . . uh . . . want to test-drive the car first?"

"No, thanks," said the vampire. "Did you park it outside?"

"Yes, sir. There's some paperwork to finish first." The salesman reminded himself that he needed the commission on this sale. His shirt was sticky with cold sweat and his hands trembled as he pushed a handful of forms across the desk.

The vampire signed his name with a flourish. "Paul Montclair."

The salesman glanced down at the forms, but his eyes were drawn, in spite of himself, to the strange face of the young man who sat on the other side of his desk. The boy looked no older than sixteen or seventeen. His skin was so white and smooth it was like bleached bone, and his dark eyes were lit with a strange violet light. The salesman licked his lips and forced himself to study the forms. "You forgot to fill in your address, sir."

"I'm moving. My current address is no good."

"If you'll just give us your new address, then. We'll need it to mail you the title."

The vampire smiled slightly. "General delivery will do fine."

The salesman mopped his brow with a handkerchief. He had noticed something peculiar about the boy's fingernails. They looked glassy against the white flesh of his fingertips. "Will you be using your old license plate?" he choked out.

"No," said the vampire. "I'll need a new one—this is how I want it to read." He wrote, "BLVDLVV."

The salesman's gaze was drawn to the page—anything rather than look at the boy's face. "Roman numerals," he observed. "Boulevard 555? Is that an address?"

"It's a private joke, actually."

"If you'll just write me a check," the salesman said hastily, "we'll be all done."

The vampire took a thick roll of cash from his pocket and peeled off hundred-dollar bills until he had paid the full price of the car. The salesman blinked at the stack of money. "We'll get you a receipt for that," he said, but he felt curiously reluctant to reach for it.

At last he forced himself to snatch the bills. He hurried off to the cashier's office, but when he returned with a receipt, the boy was gone. Out the window the salesman saw the black Jaguar backing out of its parking place. He glanced down at the pile of papers. "BLVDLVV." It hit him suddenly that it didn't stand for Boulevard 555. It said, "Blood Love." Horrified, he stared as the red taillights of the Jaguar disappeared down the dark highway.

Paul drove the Jaguar back to Georgetown. When he walked into the apartment, his father was pacing the floor. "Where've you been?" he demanded.

Paul shrugged.

"Evie's moved out!" Richard's eyes were narrowed in anger. "I thought she had only gone away for a few days, but just now I looked in her closet, and all her clothes are gone. She's taken off! She's left me!"

In the bedroom, Paul opened Evie's jewelry case and saw that it was empty. His father was right. Unless she had gone away for the weekend positively blanketed in jewels, it was a sure thing she had moved out. He walked back into the living room and picked up the telephone. No dial tone.

"I'll kill her when I get hold of her," muttered

Richard. "She can't do this to me and get away with it. I made her! She was just an ordinary housewife before I came along."

"I'm moving out myself, as a matter of fact," said Paul.

"Oh, no you don't!" His father's eyes flashed fire. "Don't give me that!"

Paul smiled. "What are you going to do?" he asked sarcastically. "Kill me?"

"Don't give me your lip, young man. I'll slap you so hard your ears will ring."

Paul flinched. It would have been smarter to sneak away the way Evie had done, but he wanted the satisfaction of telling his father off. "You think I'd stay here after the way you used Sophie to spy on me?" He folded his arms and sneered with contempt.

"I don't know what you're talking about." Richard took a step back.

"Liar," Paul spat. "Sophie as much as admitted that you put her up to spying on me. All the time I thought she loved me—" his voice faltered "—you were using her against me."

"You've got it wrong, Paul." His father sank onto the couch.

Paul had noticed that his father seemed older and smaller since Aunt Gabrielle had died. His eyes were sunken and lifeless, as if grief had robbed him of his former vitality. Or maybe it was only that Paul wasn't afraid of him anymore.

"Look at you," snarled Paul. "You're a pathetic, broken-down old vampire. I wouldn't live here with you if you paid me. I'm not surprised that Evie took off. You treated her like dirt." He rolled up his favorite jeans and tucked them under his arm. "I guess you'll just have to find somebody else to slap around now."

Richard buried his face in his hands. "Gabrielle," he whispered, "where are you?"

Paul had braced himself to be hit, but he hadn't expected this. He wondered if his father was losing his grip on reality. Gabrielle was gone forever—they both knew that.

"Gabri told me if I was ever in trouble, she had something that could help me," said Richard, tears welling in his eyes. "But now that I'm in trouble, she isn't here even to tell me what she meant."

Paul shifted his weight uncomfortably. *He* knew what his aunt had been talking about—the vampire gold she had hidden behind her fireplace. Paul had found it, but he had no intention of sharing it with his father. He hardened his voice. "Face up to the truth," he said. "I don't need you, Evie doesn't need you, and Aunt Gabrielle's dead. Good-bye, *Dad*." He turned away quickly. Richard had never been a real father to him anyway.

"Stop!" yelled Richard. "You know what Gabrielle was talking about, don't you? Tell me! I'll get it out of you." He sprang off the couch.

Paul slammed the door behind himself and ran for the emergency stairs. His heart was pounding violently. He paused just inside the fire door, breathing hard. He wished now that he hadn't come back to face his father—he should have remembered the older vampire's unnerving habit of guessing what was on his mind. Hearing the whine of the elevator, Paul sighed with relief. He was sure that by running fast he could beat his father downstairs.

Paul leapt down the stairwell and dashed into the underground parking garage. Luckily Richard didn't know about the new Jaguar. The motor roared as Paul desperately raced up the garage's ramp, speeding past the attendant's booth and breaking through the wooden barrier with a loud crack. The car shot out onto the dimly lit street. For a moment Paul heard the sound of the wooden crossbar dragging against the pavement under the car. He turned the steering wheel sharply and careened around the corner.

Just then he spotted his father on the sidewalk. Panic seized him. He stabbed the accelerator, and the car rocketed ahead. Glancing in the rearview mirror, he saw his father's dark figure running after him, shouting something incomprehensible. For a brief instant he had the horrible fear that his father was going to catch him. He ran a red light, and brakes screeched on either side of him. But the next moment he veered onto a side street, changing course, and his father vanished.

Paul sighed in relief. He was okay now.

He turned onto a wide avenue and headed

out of Georgetown. Suddenly he laughed out loud. Freedom was fizzing in his blood like champagne. The Jaguar's trunk was heavy with gold. And all of it was his!

Washington was a big city. If things worked out, his father would never find him.

When he was far from Georgetown, Paul finally slowed the car. His headlights beamed on a leather jacket and the white flash of slender legs above boots. Drawing closer, he saw it was a girl with purple hair. His mouth watered slightly. He slowed to a crawl and pulled up beside her.

"Want a ride?" he called.

The girl glanced at him. He stopped the car and flung the door open. She slid in at once, filling the car with the scent of grape Kool-Aid. Paul smiled. That must have been how she had dyed her hair. Now that he got a close look, he realized that she was younger than he was— maybe fifteen. Her face was powdered white, and her lips had been colored a startlingly dark red.

"Cool car," she said, caressing its leather seat. "Is it yours?"

Paul nodded.

"You must be rich."

Paul thought of the treasure in his trunk. "I'm not exactly poor."

"I guess you don't have any curfews or your parents telling you what you can wear."

"Not anymore." He grinned.

The girl fluffed the purple hair with one

hand. "Well, now I don't have to put up with that junk anymore either."

"You've run away?" Paul was interested.

"That's right. My parents think I'm spending the night at a girlfriend's house. I'll be in New York before they even know I'm gone. I know a boy who lives there, and he said I could stay at his place anytime." She smiled. "Maybe you'd like to drive me. I bet we could get there fast in this car."

Paul pulled the car over to the curb. "No, I'm going to take you somewhere else—some place you've never been before." His voice was soft. He twirled a strand of her hair around his forefinger and smiled, revealing his fangs. "Have you ever been with a vampire?"

Her eyes widened. He jerked the strand of hair viciously and pulled her toward him.

"That hurts," she whimpered. She kicked, and he felt her knee in his stomach. "Get away from me!" she cried, twisting desperately. "What are you? Crazy?"

Paul could sense the girl's panic and felt excitement rising in him.

"No!" she gasped. But at that moment he sank his teeth into her neck and she sagged. Her breath became a ragged rattle. He held his grip, pressing his lips tightly to the flesh and greedily gulping her blood. Warmth flooded his body. He felt lighter than air. It was as if he were hovering above the car, a black angel of death, his wings beating with the rhythm of the girl's breath. His fingertips kneaded the soft skin of her neck almost lovingly.

He realized finally that she was dead, but he felt so pleasantly warm from her blood that he couldn't make himself move. He rubbed his cheek luxuriously against her leather jacket, feeling an odd sort of tenderness toward her. Suddenly he heard laughter outside the car and stiffened. Some people were passing them on the sidewalk.

He froze until the muffled voices grew faint and disappeared altogether. Then he slid back into his own seat and regarded the girl critically. Her mouth hung open and her skin, stretched tight over the bone, looked white and lifeless. Moments ago she had been a living, breathing girl. But now she was only a tawdry corpse. He gave a sharp shove to her shoulders and let her fall forward with her head hanging between her knees. Now he wouldn't have to look at her face, and she wouldn't be visible out the car window.

He started up the car and drove slowly, checking for alleys or side streets. At last he saw a Dumpster in the shadows. Scanning the area to make sure no one was coming, he got out and dragged the body out of the car. He hoisted it over his head and jackknifed it, headfirst, into the Dumpster. Her body sank into the garbage with a soft thump.

Paul turned away without interest and put the top of his car down. As he drove away, he felt warm with human blood, but somehow vaguely unsatisfied. It was hard to put his finger on what was wrong. He supposed he had wanted not just blood, but everything that made the girl human—her breath, her heart, her soul. It was a hunger that could not be satisfied. He frowned, feeling a sharp pang of loneliness.

Ari. He squeezed his eyes shut for a second, chasing the image of his twin out of his mind. Only the throb of the car's powerful engine comforted him. He did have his car, he reminded himself. That was something.

He gazed at the long shining hood stretching out before him. Buying the Jaguar had been easier than he'd thought it would be. It had taken only one call to a well-known South African collector to convert one of Aunt Gabrielle's gold chalices into cash. Paul had told the collector that his name was Jessie Driscoll. He smiled now, thinking of how he had used the name of a classmate who had tried to kill him. What an irony!

Paul realized he was on a road outside the city now. He was a little vague about how he had gotten there. He drove as if in a dream, feeling all alone in the world—as if he had killed the last living human being on earth. The road was empty. Frost-covered pumpkin fields stretched into the distance on either side of him. All of a sudden he heard a rooster's crow. He glanced uneasily at the sky. The night was still black, but gooseflesh rose on his arms. The rooster sensed, as he did, that morning was twitching at the horizon. Before long, he would need to find a place to hide.

CHAPTER
TWO

ARI MONTCLAIR STARED AT THE BLACKENED RUIN OF her aunt's mansion. She wore a wool scarf wrapped around her head, casting her eyes into deep shadow. The scarf was not much of a disguise, but on this moonlit night it would do. She knew she shouldn't have come here—but she hadn't been able to stop herself.

Paul. She hadn't seen her brother since the night of the fire. Her longing for him was so fierce it seemed the sheer force of her will might make him come running out the door—only, the door was a heap of ashes. Where once an elegant mansion had stood, now only a pile of charred wood lay in the shadow of a shattered brick facade.

Paul had vanished into the darkness with their father that night. Why had she come back, half expecting to find him here where she had left him? It made no sense. Yet she was comforted somehow, staring at the black ruin. She wasn't sure why, but when she was here, Paul seemed closer.

Ari gazed around her. The garage looked relatively undamaged. She wondered if by chance the basement had escaped the fire as well. Her mother's belongings had been stored there. Or had every last memento of her former life been consumed?

Ari climbed the front steps and peered through the scorched remnants of the door. The black-and-white marble of the hallway was smeared with ashes, but it seemed as if the floor might offer a firm footing. She stepped inside and her footsteps crunched in the eerie silence. Suddenly she noticed there were a number of gaps in the marble. It would be too dangerous to try to get into the basement. Her heart sank. Not that it even really mattered—her mother's possessions had probably been soaked and destroyed by the firemen's hoses.

But as Ari turned to leave, a flash of light caught her eye. Glancing toward the living room, she saw that something shiny and metallic lay on the floor. She picked her way carefully through the hall, past the sodden skeleton of what had once been the couch. All at once she gasped. A glittering golden chalice was half-buried in the ashes. She recognized it at once—it was from Aunt Gabrielle's hidden treasure.

Ari immediately glanced over at the fireplace, which stood at the base of the broken facade. The mantel had been pulled away from the wall! Someone had ransacked the secret store of gold! The mantel's marble face was dark, and a long black crack showed along its side.

The thief must have dropped this one cup. She picked it off the floor and rubbed it against her jeans legs, then tilted it to let the moonlight dance on its smooth, oval jewels. A vague dread seized her. *Vampire gold . . .*

Biting her lip, she stuffed the chalice into her jacket pocket. She reminded herself that Aunt Gabrielle had once used it to save Paul's life. She couldn't leave it for a stranger to find.

Moving quickly, Ari climbed down from the house and made her way over to the garage. The entire place smelled like damp charcoal. Part of the roof was gone. Standing inside, she could see the moon sailing overhead in the company of dark clouds. For some reason Aunt Gabrielle's Mercedes was gone, while the twins' Mazda was still parked in the garage. Had the thief who'd stolen the vampire gold taken the Mercedes as well?

Ari jingled her keys in her pocket. It would be so easy for her to drive the Mazda away. Suddenly she pulled open the garage door. Without thinking too deeply about what she was doing, she slid in behind the wheel and backed the car out onto the street, a dull loneliness settling over her like a thick fog.

Paul—where are you?

With one hand she pulled the scarf off her head and took a deep breath. The car sped toward Wisconsin Avenue. Everyone thought she had died in the fire, and now she was as rootless and as aimless as a spirit. Out of habit she turned onto Dunbarton Street. Sybil's house looked cozy and brightly lit in the moonlight. She could see inside the uncurtained windows of the house, but no one inside the house could see her. Exactly as if she were a ghost.

Her eyes were drawn up to the lighted windows of Sybil's bedroom. Two shadows were pacing back and forth. All at once Ari spotted a familiar car parked at the curb. Cos! His image came so vividly to her mind that she gasped—his sunlit brown eyes, the carelessly rumpled hair. He was here! It would be so easy to see them both right now . . . but she knew she couldn't give way to that impulse. It was far too dangerous. She did not even dare to glance a second time at the bedroom window. She was afraid she might change her mind. *It's better if they think I'm dead,* she thought. The car rolled slowly past the house and into the night.

"Ari has got to be dead," Cos said. "If she were alive, she'd have called to let me know. It's time I faced it, Sybil. She's dead."

Sybil sat down on her bed and crossed her legs, shaking her frizzy red hair out of her face.

"I think she and Paul escaped. In fact, I'm sure of it."

Cos shook his head. "You've seen the house. Nobody could have survived that fire." He fiddled with a brush on the dressing table, and Sybil could see his troubled face reflected in its mirror. "I've asked my parents to let me transfer to another school," he said.

Sybil lifted her eyebrow a fraction of an inch. "You're halfway through your junior year. You can't transfer now. Where would you go?"

"I don't care—I can't take staying at St. Anselm's. I keep wondering which kids were in the mob that killed Ari. You're the only one I can talk to, Syb. I know you didn't have anything to do with it." His face darkened. "Every time I see Jessie I go cold all over. You can bet he was one of the ringleaders. I swear if I get ahold of him, I . . . I might . . I'm afraid of what I'm going to do to him."

"Cos, don't say things like that," Sybil said anxiously. "I'm sure Paul and Ari are okay. Didn't you hear that the police didn't find any bodies?"

"Maybe the fire vaporized them." Cos's face was bleak. "Maybe there's nothing left."

Sybil shook her head. "I'm sure they're both okay. I'm positive of it."

"Why?" Cos grabbed her shoulders and stared intently into her eyes. "Why are you so sure? You know something, don't you? You couldn't sit there looking so cool if you didn't. You've heard from Ari!"

Sybil gulped and nodded.

Cos went pale suddenly. "You *have* heard from her. My God." His arms fell to his sides.

"Not exactly." Sybil avoided his eyes. "I mean I haven't talked to her, but my brother Rab has. The night of the fire she called him and asked him for help. He got her out of town, but you've got to promise me to keep it a secret, Cos. I shouldn't have told you."

Cos fell into a chair. He was absolutely white with shock. "Ari called Rab!" he choked. "Why didn't she call me?"

"You won't tell anybody, will you?" Sybil's voice rose. "The mob already tried to kill them once, and they might try it again. You won't let on, will you?"

"Don't worry. I won't interfere in Ari's new life."

Sybil glanced at him uneasily. The words were right, but the tone sounded all wrong.

"She let me think she was dead," Cos went on bitterly. "I wouldn't do that to my worst enemy. She let me think she was *dead!* Would it have killed her to pick up the phone and let me know she was okay?"

"Please don't tell anybody!" Sybil pleaded.

"Where is she?" A dangerous light gleamed in his eyes.

Sybil shook her head. "I don't know. Rab said she was starting life over in another state. Paul's gone to live with his dad."

"I bet I can guess where she is." Cos closed

his eyes and ran his fingers through his hair. "Rab! I might have known."

Downstairs in the Barrons' study, Rab sat in a wide leather chair and glanced uneasily at Mr. Barron. "Can a dead person's estate be settled if there's no body?" he asked.

"That depends." Mr. Barron removed his glasses and polished the lenses. "There must be a determination of death, prima facie evidence, as it were."

Rab had heard lawyers' language all his life, and he had no trouble figuring out that meant "maybe."

"What would it take?" asked Rab.

"Evidence of foul play, a police report indicating death. In short, witnesses to the death or some other evidence that satisfies the police."

"What if the only person willing to testify to the death is an heir of the estate?"

"No problem." Mr. Barron placed the glasses on his round face and turned an inscrutable gaze on Rab. "Action on an estate is usually brought by the heirs. No one else has an interest in settling the estate, after all. But may I ask why all this sudden interest in estates?"

"I think you can guess," said Rab. He knew he shouldn't have let Sybil know Ari was alive. But he hadn't been able to bear Sybil's pain when she had called him weeping on the night of the fire. Unfortunately he had little doubt

19

that she had already spilled the news to their parents.

"Why don't you tell me yourself," suggested Mr. Barron.

Rab clasped his hands behind his back and gazed out the window into the darkness. "Ari Montclair is staying with me—and that's gotten tricky, because she doesn't like taking my money. She's even talking about getting a job, which would be stupid, because she'll have a hard enough time finishing high school the way it is." Rab turned his eyes back to Mr. Barron's stout, distinguished form. "I'm sure Ari has a legal claim on her aunt's estate, and if she can get at it, at least that would solve the money problem."

Mr. Barron put his hands together and looked thoughtfully over his fingertips. "Rab, I wouldn't—" he began, then he paused. "Are you certain Gabrielle Montclair died in that fire? The police found no body, you know."

"She's dead, all right. Ari watched that mob burn her alive."

Mr. Barron winced. "Ari must go to the police, of course."

"She won't. I've asked her to and she flatly refuses."

Mr. Barron fixed an unflinching gaze on Rab. "I hear her brother murdered those two girls at Sybil's school. Is that true?"

Rab hesitated. "Yes."

"So that's why the mob of kids stormed the house," said Mr. Barron softly. "I'd heard rumors, but I didn't know what to make of them. All sorts of wild tales are going around." He raised an eyebrow. "I've even heard that kids are swearing that all the Montclairs are vampires." He flashed a humorless smile.

Rab got out of his chair and walked over to the window.

"Listen, Rab. I don't want you getting involved in this," Mr. Barron said suddenly. "The police are investigating the fire, and the entire story is likely to come out sooner or later. Furthermore, that boy will kill again—you can count on it. Serial killers rarely stop unless they're caught. That means Ari's going to find herself in the middle of a nasty court case. She may be facing possible charges as an accessory. Her picture will be splashed all over the newspapers. It's going to be a big sordid mess. My advice is to stay clear of it."

"Too late, I'm afraid," said Rab. "I'm already in it up to my neck."

Mr. Barron looked at him for a long time. Finally he said, "I assume Ari is having nothing to do with her brother."

"No, she's made a complete break. He doesn't even know where she is."

"That's something, anyway." Mr. Barron sighed. "Does she even know where the boy is hiding?"

Rab shrugged. "With his father, I think."

Mr. Barron grimaced. "We'll have to hope that his father can keep him out of trouble."

CHAPTER
THREE

PAUL KNOCKED ON THE DOOR OF THE GEORGETOWN apartment where Verena lived. He didn't even know her last name, but in a strange and twisted way they were close—as close as two people could get.

The door opened and a slender blond girl faced him. A dimple teased the corner of her mouth, and her skin, though pale, was flawless. A tiny diamond earring glittered in each white earlobe. "Paul!" she cried. "Long time no see. Come in."

Verena often used old-fashioned expressions. That wasn't surprising—in actual years she was closer to Paul's father's age than his own. But she looked sixteen, and her silver dress, slit up the thigh, revealed a breathtaking stretch of leg. "I didn't expect you," she said, glancing at him under her lashes. "I thought you and Sophie had something going."

Sophie's name was like a knife in Paul's stomach, but he forced his face to remain expressionless. He was sure Verena was deliberately trying to cause him pain. "Sophie's history," he said steadily. "She never even crosses my mind."

Verena caressed his cheek with a cold hand and gazed up at him with a smile. "You're so cute when you lie," she said.

"Can I stay here with you?" he asked.

She chuckled low in her throat. "Sure, love, anytime. Remember how you got down on your knees and begged me to hide you? I loved that. I always think vampires are so cute when they're brand new."

Paul swept his arm back suddenly. The vicious blow caught Verena in the face, and for a moment she looked surprised. Then she started laughing. "Don't play too rough, or maybe I won't let you stay."

In a haze of red anger he grabbed her and shook her uncontrollably. Her head snapped back and forth, and the silken fringe of her fair hair flew over her face. "You did this to me," he whispered through clenched teeth. "You made me this way."

"Liar. You wanted it," she taunted. "You told me you wanted to live forever. You did! Besides, I couldn't *make* you drink my blood. Nobody can make a person do that."

Paul sank down onto the couch and covered his face with his hands. "Jeez," he said thickly.

He put his hand to his neck as if to fend off the memory of that sharp pain—the moment she had bit him. As if it were yesterday he remembered her cold lips pressing against his neck and the terrible suction. He had been too weak to move or even breathe. Maybe he had muttered something about wanting to live forever—he wasn't sure. But he was clear about the viciousness of her bite. The pain had been like a burning iron pressed against the flesh. The memory of the loud gurgling of his blood welling in her throat sickened him even now. He had been too weak to draw away from her when she pressed her bleeding wrist to his mouth. It hadn't been his fault!

He gazed at Verena dully. "I hate you," he said.

She examined her nails, smiling. "I always knew we were going to be close."

"Did you hear me!" he shouted. "I hate you!"

She strolled over to a dresser on top of which sat an open jewelry box. She pawed through the heaps of beads and bracelets aimlessly. "Don't you think about me a lot?" she asked.

"Yes!" he cried. "All I can think about is how I can get back at you."

She draped a strand of beads around her neck and smiled provocatively. "And when somebody mentions my name, doesn't your heart beat faster so you feel kind of sick?"

"Yeah," he said, his eyes narrowing. "But it's because I want to hurt you."

"See?" She giggled merrily, twirling the beads around her fingers. "It's like I'm the center of your life. That's the way it is—the person you hate becomes *important*. Haven't you noticed?"

Only the painful thinness of her arms and the strange emerald glow of her eyes gave away the fact that she was a vampire. She could have fooled him. He had known the truth about her, yet he had gone off with her anyway. Why? He wasn't sure of that even now. "What are you getting at?" he demanded.

"All I'm saying is that hate is really strong." Verena shrugged. "Like where is Sophie now in your life? Nowhere. You said yourself she's nothing to you anymore." She held out her arms. "Here you are—with me!" She suddenly spun around and around, laughing. Her fair hair flew out as she whirled on the gleaming floor and fell into Paul's arms.

She threw her head back, and Paul could see the long blue line of the artery in her throat. Unable to stop himself, he struck, digging his fangs in deeply above the soft hollow at the base of the neck. Her ragged cry of pain excited him, and suddenly he pushed her down on the floor and struck again, his tongue rasping against her flesh until a thin stream of her blood jetted against the back of his throat—the delicate, intoxicating wash of vampire blood. He closed his eyes so he didn't have to see her face.

"You hate me," Verena whispered. "Remember how you hate me!"

He was aware that Verena's hair was tickling his cheek, and all at once he felt a dull pain. When he opened his eyes he saw that her long curved fangs had sunk into his neck. He put a hand up to fend her off, but she caught his hand in hers. Her grip was surprisingly strong. Her smiling lips glistened with his blood. She took his finger in his mouth and sucked, and a sudden shudder shook him. He felt as if she had drained the strength from him. Her fair hair flew in his face in her sudden frenzy.

He must have blacked out then, because the next thing he knew he was lying on the rug with Verena's head resting on his chest. She was snoring lightly. Her blond hair was matted with blood.

Anxiously he put his hand to his neck, but to his relief it felt okay. If it weren't for the weakness he felt, he might almost have thought he had imagined what had happened—it had seemed so unreal, so dreamlike. "Get up!" he said harshly.

Verena blinked, then rolled off onto the shaggy rug. "Yikes, I'm a mess." She scrambled to her feet. "How time flies when you're having fun."

"You're lucky you didn't kill me," said Paul.

She laughed. "I can't kill you, love. You're a vampire, remember?"

"Did you get enough of my blood?" Paul

27

asked sarcastically. "You're a pig."

"Oh, I never get enough vampire blood." She grinned. "It's sort of like Chinese food. You're hungry again an hour later." She heaped her matted hair on top of her head with one hand and flashed her long, curved fangs. "I've got to shower. I can never sleep when I'm all yucky like this."

Paul cast a startled glance at the window. Dawn was near. That meant he would have to share Verena's coffin.

Verena shimmied out of her dress. It was stained with his watery blood. "I have to keep switching dry cleaners, because they always look at me so funny when I bring my stuff in. My cleaning bills are awful."

She stood naked before him. He could see her hipbones bulging under her blue-white flesh and a line of ribs under her breasts. Paul didn't trust her an inch. But there was a good side to that, he thought ruefully. There was no way she could let him down. Verena could never hurt him the way Sophie had.

He pulled a comb out of his pocket and ran it through his hair, checking his reflection in an oval mirror on the wall. "Verena, you don't have to answer this, but I'm curious." He turned around to face her. "Do you have any hobbies outside of shopping and ruining other people's lives?"

"Sure," she said. "Old movies. Of course, I do get tired of movies—but I never get tired of making pretty young boys into vampires." She flicked a finger under his chin. "You're so cute."

He brushed her hand away. "You . . . you're disgusting," he said.

She reached for a robe and wrapped it around her painfully thin body. "Isn't that funny." She giggled. "Most boys are crazy about the way I look." She walked toward the bathroom, but hesitated and turned around. "Hey, I saw somebody you know the other day."

Paul's heart leapt painfully in his chest. Sophie! Verena had seen her—

"Evangeline Wingate." Verena sucked on a strand of hair. "Evie moved out on Richard, you know. I was surprised to see she's still around. If I left Richard, I would get as far away as I could."

"Where is Evie?"

The corners of Verena's eyes crinkled with laughter. "She's moved in with Dubay. Isn't that a hoot? I mean, Dubay is such a slob—fungus on his toothbrush, moldy old sneakers under the sofa. And Evie is pathologically neat. Personally I'm convinced that's why Richard wanted her. He needed someone to do his laundry. She has absolutely no personality otherwise. Who would want somebody like that hanging around their neck for eternity?"

"I like Evie," said Paul. "She's nice."

Verena laughed. "You share your father's taste. Kinda like with you and him and Sophie, huh? A threesome? I hear you and your dad both went for Sophie, too."

Paul stepped blindly toward Verena, but she slammed the bathroom door in his face. He could hear her peals of laughter over the running water. He banged on the door.

"Get lost!" yelled Verena. "Go soak your head!"

"What's Dubay's phone number?" Paul called. "Do you know?"

"Of course I know." The water stopped running abruptly. "Why?"

"Dad's threatened to kill Evie. I think I'd better warn her."

"I've got his number in the drawer of my desk somewhere," she said, turning the shower back on.

Paul strode over to the desk. Once he might have laughed at his father's threats. After all, he had been told often enough that vampires were immortal. But now he had seen how easily fire could consume that thread of immortality. He would never forget the sight of his aunt Gabrielle burning into nothingness before his eyes. It was all too easy for him to imagine his father putting a torch to Evie. He had to warn her!

The desk drawer was full of old letters, photographs, souvenirs, and spiral-bound notebooks. Shuffling through the odds and ends, Paul suddenly gasped. There was a picture of Ari and him in there! "Merry Christmas," said the glossy card. It was a reprint of a snapshot taken a couple of years ago. His mother had signed her name at the bottom of the card, and the sudden memory of her brought an uncontrollable tear to his eyes. She had always wanted to take a snapshot whenever he and Ari got dressed up.

In the photo Ari was beautiful, her black hair tumbling in curls to the shoulders of a slender black dress. They had been happy then. He remembered games of chess on lazy summer days and the sweet mulberries that grew just outside their porch. During the long New Orleans summers, it seemed their lips had always been purple with berry juice.

Looking at the snapshot now, he scarcely recognized himself. It wasn't that he had aged much. Vampires didn't age. But something important had changed inside him.

He heard the bathroom door open and turned to face Verena. "Where did you get this?" he demanded.

"I stole it." Her wet hair was streaming down her thin shoulders, and the bathrobe was damp. "Gabrielle had it out on a table when she had a big Christmas party. I liked your looks, so I took it. I had a feeling I'd get a chance at you someday when you came to visit her."

She rummaged in the open desk drawer. "I always try to get a little something from the guys I make into vampires. Kind of a souvenir, you know?" She tossed a heavy class ring onto the desk. Its purple jewel gleamed in the lamplight. "This one was sweet. Kevin was his name. See the initials inside? K. A. W. He had the cutest freckles."

"What happened to him?"

She frowned. "I don't think he has freckles now. Vampire skin is different. And of course, now he can't go out in the sun."

A sudden memory flashed through Paul's mind of him and Ari stretched out side by side on a float in the lake, squinting at the clouds drifting lazily in the bright sky overhead.

The sunshine, too, was a thing of the past.

Verena toweled her hair vigorously. "Oh," she cried. "Look at that!" She fished a cocktail napkin out of the drawer. Someone had scrawled, "I love you," in one corner of it. "That guy's name was Pete, I think." She frowned. "I was afraid he was going to be clingy. You know, the type of boy who never lets you have any time to yourself."

"What happened to him?"

"He's dead." She looked at him blankly. "He wouldn't do it. Boy, was I surprised!" She dropped the paper napkin in the wastebasket.

"That's what I should have done," said Paul in a low voice.

"You're kidding me!" exclaimed Verena. "You mean you'd rather be dead? Why? Man, vampires have it all!" She tossed the towel aside. "I hate to go to sleep with my hair wet, but that's the way it goes sometimes." She glanced at the window nervously. "We better hurry. I hear the dawn."

32

Verena's bedroom was dark. Paul could scarcely make out her coffin lying on the floor as he followed her in. He heard the top open with a clunk, and then he saw the long white oval of its white satin lining. "Cozy, huh?" she said, lying down. "Come on, Paul. Don't take all night!"

He felt sick as he lowered himself onto her. Her full breasts flattened under his weight, and he felt a wet strand of her hair stick to his cheek. "Bombs away!" cried Verena. The coffin's lid fell closed. Verena's breath stank of blood. His yearning for his twin overwhelmed him in the blackness.

"Ari," Paul groaned. "Where are you?"

CHAPTER
FOUR

"I CAN'T BELIEVE YOU BROUGHT THE CAR BACK here!" Rab exclaimed.

Ari sat in silence, hands clutched in her lap, staring at the long, thin line of Rab's lips. They were curved down in anger. Sun streaming through the open window of his Charlottesville apartment made his frizzy black hair glisten.

"A car is simple to trace," he snapped. "You're only making it easy for your father and Paul to find you. Is that what you want?"

Ari couldn't give him the truthful answer— that she didn't know what she wanted anymore. "I need a car," she mumbled. "And my own was just sitting in the garage. I couldn't resist driving off with it. So shoot me."

Rab sighed and ran his fingers through his hair. "I only want to protect you, Ari. You know that. I want what's best for you."

"I know." She leapt up and paced the floor. "But having you drive me everywhere makes me feel like a six-year-old. I need that car, Rab! If I can't be free to come and go as I want, I might just as well be dead."

"You don't know what you're saying," he protested.

"Besides, now that I've got the car I can get a job," Ari went on quickly, "and I won't have to take money from you anymore."

"You know I don't mind about the money. Anyway, I think I see a way out of that. I've talked to my dad." Rab's lips twitched. "My *other* dad, I mean. Turns out you can put in a claim for your aunt's estate based on a police report. All we've got to do is go to the police and tell them what happened."

"I can't go to the police." Ari collapsed onto the futon and stared up at him helplessly.

"Why not? You don't even know where Paul is, so talking to the cops can't put him in danger. Once you tell the police the truth about what happened the night of the fire, we can put legal wheels in motion and get hold of your aunt's money."

"Probably none of it goes to me anyway."

"Some of it does." Rab coughed. "It's irregular, but Dad pulled in some IOUs and found out it's been left in equal shares to Gabrielle's survivors—you, Paul, and Richard. There's no reason why you can't lay your hands on your share."

"It's probably not much, anyway," said Ari stubbornly. "Why bother?"

"Oh, come on! If there wasn't any money worth talking about, your aunt wouldn't have lived in a mansion in Georgetown! What's going on with you, Ari?" asked Rab. "You aren't making any sense."

"I'm afraid to go to the police."

Rab took a deep breath. "Okay, it's scary. But you haven't done anything wrong, so the police can't hurt you."

Her eyes widened.

"Not *very* wrong, anyway," he went on hastily. "The police don't know you helped Paul move Susannah's body. How could they? All you're talking to them about is the fire. No problem!"

"Have you thought about this—I can't risk having them arrest anybody for setting that fire! What if those kids get up on the stand and swear that Paul is a vampire?"

"That would be bad." Rab's eyes softened. "And I'm not advising you to lie, understand. But you *could* say that you didn't get a chance to recognize anybody that night. That way, there would be no way the police could make an arrest."

"Would the cops believe me if I said that, though?" She shivered.

"Why not? Your story is you couldn't see very well from where you were standing on the staircase, and you can't be sure about the voices."

37

"I'll never forget them," said Ari in a low voice.

He shook his head. "They sounded vaguely familiar, that's all."

Ari fell back against the cushions. "I can't be sure," she repeated numbly.

"You're going to do fine with the cops. It'll be a piece of cake."

Ari hoped he was right. She stared at him. Ever since Rab had told her that he was her half brother, she had found herself noticing family resemblance. He had a beaked nose like Paul's; he was tall and dark like all the Montclairs. But most of all, he had that strange second sense—that peculiar ability that was both the gift and the curse of the family. But for some reason, Rab still didn't feel like her brother. Not at all.

"Tomorrow we'll take the car in and have it painted," he said.

Ari smiled a little. Rab *was* high-handed—just like the other Montclair men. But she wouldn't tell him that. He might be insulted. After all, the two of them were still practically strangers.

Once Rab had gone to bed, Ari took the gold chalice out from her drawer. She had stashed it there under some stacks of underwear. After the way Rab had yelled at her for bringing back the car, she had no intention of telling him about the chalice. Keeping it was much more scary than keeping the car, but it was such a strong link to her past that she felt fiercely possessive of it in a way she couldn't explain—she *needed* it. She peered at its rough-cut jewels and the intricate, grotesque engravings of birds of prey tearing at their victims. The cup was smeared with ashes, and Ari polished it with the corner of her shirt to get a better look.

Suddenly she heard Paul's voice. "Ari!" he cried.

In an instant the blood drained from her face. She looked over her shoulder. No one was there. She rose and tiptoed to the apartment's front door. Peering through the peephole, she saw that no one was outside. Her heart was thumping violently. Was she losing her mind? Had she imagined her twin's voice?

All at once she was anxious to get the chalice out of sight. But when she picked it up, the jewels swam in her sight, and her vision grew dim, as if she were about to faint. Paul's face shimmered before her. Ari gasped and reached out to touch him, but she felt her hand go right through his image and touch the warm gold of the chalice.

"Ari, I need you." His mouth moved slightly ahead of the words, like a movie out of sync. Ari's eyes grew large. The gold chalice seemed to be acting as some sort of transmitter!

"Remember the mist rising from the swamp and the hot summer mornings?" his image said softly. "You and me barefoot, sticky with sweat and with our mosquito bites itching. We used to go slipping and sliding on the muddy banks. We were scared, because we knew we weren't supposed to go messing around back there. I wish we were there now. I wish I could put my arms around you and hold you close to my beating heart. I miss you so much." His eyes closed, and his dark lashes lay like shadows on his cheeks.

Slowly the image faded. Ari shook the chalice and rubbed the gold with the tail of her shirt—but it was no use. She could not conjure him up again. For several minutes Ari clutched the chalice to her breast, reluctant to put it away. What did Paul's sudden silence mean? Her heart squeezed in fear. Was he dead?

The next morning, fatigue made the skin under Ari's eyes appear swollen and bruised. But after a sleepless night she had come to the conclusion that Paul could not be dead. Vampires did not die peacefully—she was convinced of that. They were tortured by the sun until they died in agony, as Paul nearly did once. Or they went up in flames like Aunt Gabrielle. And if Paul had tried to contact her once, she was certain he would try again.

Ari offered no argument when Rab told her that they were going to a body shop to get the car painted. When they arrived, a man in white overalls surveyed the Mazda doubtfully. "Don" was embroidered in red script over his pocket, and he held a clipboard under one arm. "I don't get why you want to paint it," he said. "It's brand new and there isn't a scratch on it."

"We want a different color," said Rab.

Don scratched his head. "Well, it's up to you, but it's going to cost you, and the thing is, it's not good for the car. We've got to sand it down, you see? That opens up all the rust pores hidden under the paint. After that the car rusts that much easier. See what I mean?"

"Paint it burgundy," said Rab.

The man frowned. "What happened to its license plate?"

"It got stolen," said Rab. "We're going to order a new one."

The man shook his head. "Hey, this isn't a police thing, is it? I mean, hit-and-run or drugs or something like that? Because we're supposed to report anything suspicious."

"No—of course not." Rab smiled, but his voice was unconvincing. "We just don't like the color."

The man ran his fingers over the headlights as if checking for shreds of a pedestrian. Finally, he frowned. "Well, it's your funeral. You can pick it up on Friday."

That evening, a loud knock brought Sophie Allenby to the front door of her Washington apartment. A tall vampire pushed his way in. "Where is Paul?" he demanded.

"He's not here."

The vampire slapped her. "Don't lie to me! You're hiding him."

Sophie whimpered, clutching her hand to her stinging cheek. "I don't know, Richard. I told you."

Richard strode into the bedroom and threw open the closet. He began pulling her clothes off hangers and throwing them to the floor. She wondered if she should run out of the apartment. But that would only convince him she had something to hide.

He bent over her coffin. She saw him open it, kneel beside it, and sniff at its satin lining. A moment later he stood facing her, his eyes narrowed and his thumb and forefinger pinched together. "This is his hair," he said between clenched teeth. "He slept here yesterday, didn't he?"

"That's not his hair. It's mine!" cried Sophie. "Paul has never been here. Never!"

Richard flung the strand aside. "If he's not here you must know where he is. Tell me!"

"We parted on bad terms," Sophie said. "I don't have any idea where he is. Believe me, I'm the last person he'd come to. Why are you so anxious to find him all of a sudden?"

"He's stolen something of mine," said Richard.

Sophie looked at him in blank surprise. She had never heard of Richard having any possessions beyond a car and expensive clothes. "What on earth did he steal from you?"

Richard's eyes darkened. "I'm not really sure."

Sophie swallowed. She had heard rumors that Richard had become unstable since his sister's death—but this seemed completely insane.

Richard fell onto the sofa. "It's something of Gabrielle's," he said. "I'm not sure exactly what, but it will help me. I know it will. Gabrielle promised me she would give it to me if I ever needed it." He picked up a vase that sat on the coffee table.

She wished he would put down the fragile porcelain, but she was afraid to speak. Richard's eyes were as cold and dark as stones.

"I'm going to wring the truth out of Paul and make him give it back to me," he said. "Where is he, Sophie?"

"Truly, Richard, I don't know."

Richard suddenly threw the vase at a mirror across the room. Glass exploded everywhere, shattering the silence. Sophie bit her lip.

"You lie," said Richard. "All vampires lie. I can't trust anybody now that Gabrielle's dead."

Sophie shrugged. "I hope you find what you're looking for," she lied.

"Sure, sure, you do." He smiled. "I know that. Come here, Sophie." He patted the couch beside him.

"No!" She cowered against the door. It was too late now to make a break for it. She knew from bitter experience that she couldn't outrun him.

"Come here!" His eyes flashed. "Don't make me force you or you'll be sorry."

Sophie sat down. She hated that Richard had a hold on her. It was as if his image were somehow burned into her heart. She clenched her fists so tightly that her nails bit into her palms. "Remember the night we first met?" he asked.

"Not really," lied Sophie. She could feel him nibbling playfully at her neck, and a scream rose in her throat. She gulped hard and clamped her mouth shut, refusing to let the scream escape. She couldn't show her fear.

"I remember," Richard said. "We were at a poetry reading. I love poetry readings." He chuckled softly. "So many sensitive young girls and some exceptionally attractive boys as well— all of them hungry for experience."

"Yes," said Sophie, remembering suddenly that Richard had seemed sophisticated to her. Her friends had been staring at her with open envy when Sophie had slipped on the back of Richard's motorcycle. The bike had roared through the dark countryside, its vibration rattling her teeth and its engine deafening her. Suddenly Richard had veered off the road. Then he'd stopped its motor and let it fall to the ground. When its headlight had gone out, Sophie had felt a sudden sick feeling in her stomach.

Her eyes closed as she relived the moment. . . .

"Richard?"

It was so dark in the pasture that she could scarcely see him. Only the whites of his eyes and his teeth were visible. "Say some lines of poetry," he said, lying on the ground beside her. "Keats?" he suggested. "I adore Keats. 'Here lies one whose name was writ on water.' That was what he wrote for his epitaph. But his name wasn't written on water the way he thought—he became immortal."

She felt a twinge of panic—then shame. It made her feel like a child. But being alone with Richard in the dark scared her. "Take me home," she said.

Richard sprung up from the ground in an instant. He moved like a cat—suddenly she could smell him beside her and feel his breath. "No, no, darling," he murmured. "You want to taste life, don't you?"

"No, I want to go home." She leapt up and ran as fast as she could.

But it was no use. She was gasping with painful heaves of exhaustion when she became aware that he was beside her, scarcely breathing at all. Richard had caught up with her easily. She felt him lay his cool hand on her shoulder, and she cringed as she felt his hand ruffle her hair. But the pain in her lungs told her she was too winded to run any farther.

"If you hurt me," she panted desperately, "I'll kick you."

His low chuckle, so surprisingly close to her ear, sent chills up her spine. "Come on, little girl," he said softly. "Don't you want to be immortal?"

"Well, yes, but—" she began, but sudden sharp pain in her neck abruptly cut her off. Suddenly she was pressed to the ground, trapped by his weight, gasping with fear. His greasy hair brushed against her cheek. Struggling, she felt his cold wet lips against her flesh and the pain grew. She heard a low groan and realized with horror that the scarcely human voice she heard was her own. A slurping noise sounded in her ear. Her clothes were wet—her warm blood was jetting out of her body with every heartbeat. But the most horrifying thing was that she felt his weight pressing her to the ground, but she couldn't see him at all. He was a black shape over her, blocking the stars.

Finally she heard his voice saying, "You aren't ready to die yet, are you? You need some of my blood—yours is almost gone. Drink, pretty one, drink."

She was so thirsty—more thirsty than she had ever been. Something wet was pressing against her mouth. It tasted like wine. . . . Then everything had gone black.

"A penny for your thoughts," said Richard, and Sophie's vivid memories scattered. She turned to look at him sitting beside her on the couch, a tall dark vampire, his eyes glittering with evil. Was this, she wondered, what she had taken for sophistication, so long ago?

"You know what I'm thinking," said Sophie. "You took advantage of me."

"You flatter me. Nobody made you become a vampire." Richard stood up and stretched.

Sophie had heard that line a hundred times. "Nobody made you do it." It was standard among vampires. But she didn't buy it. Where was free will when you were close to death and almost unconscious?

"You murdered me," she said. "All the lies in the world can't change that."

Richard glanced around the living room, a slow smile widening his mouth. "How can you say I murdered you? I could have left you dead, but I shared my blood with you instead. And here you are in this pretty apartment with all eternity stretching before you. You are splendidly lucky, Sophie, and you're ungrateful for all I've given you."

She regarded him stonily. Odd—when she had been in high school she hadn't fit in, and now that she was a vampire, she didn't fit in any better. *Splendidly lucky?*

"I know I can count on you to let me know if you hear from Paul," purred Richard.

"Of course." Sophie's mouth curved into a smile, but the smile did not reach her eyes.

Richard paused at the door. "If you don't know where he is, I'll bet I know who does—that sister of his." He clenched his fists. "I need to get my hands on her and bind her to me so she can't escape." He smiled. "And I think I know how to do that, don't you, Sophie?"

She gazed into his eyes and her blood ran cold.

"The mistake I made with Paul," he went on

softly, "is that I let him find his own way. Now look at how he repays me—stealing what is mine. I won't make that mistake with Ari."

"How are you going to find her?" asked Sophie.

Richard's eyes narrowed. "Why do you want to know? So you can tell Paul, I guess."

"I told you I don't know where Paul is," she said.

"I'll find Ari. And sure as death, she will lead me to Paul." Richard laughed and closed the door behind him.

As soon as she was sure he was gone, Sophie began packing.

She would never come back.

CHAPTER
FIVE

"DUBAY? THIS IS PAUL MONTCLAIR." PAUL HELD THE telephone receiver with his chin. On a spiral-bound pad he was sketching a cone-shaped volcano that was spurting clouds, looking as if it might erupt any minute. "Can I speak to Evie?"

"She's not here. What gave you the idea she was with me?"

Paul rolled his eyes. "If she's not there, that's good," he said. "Because my father says he's going to kill her, and I think he's serious."

"Hang on," said Dubay.

Paul heard some muffled sounds, then Evie's frightened voice. "Paul? Does he know where I am?"

"Not from me, Evie. But your location isn't exactly a big secret. Verena knew where you were. That's how I got your number."

He heard her gasp. "What am I going to do?" she cried.

"Ship out to Montana?" Paul suggested lightly. "Or maybe Bombay. The farther away the better."

"Richard will find me wherever I go." Evie's voice trembled. "I can't explain it—but you must know. You're his son. If he touches me, I have to go with him. It's horrible!"

Paul shivered. He had had his own experience with his father's hypnotic touch. "Stay out of his reach," advised Paul. "He's really mad."

"Completely, utterly, totally," said Evie with vehemence.

Paul realized Evie thought he meant mad in the British sense—insane. He started to correct her, but then he stopped. Maybe she was right about his dad being insane. "By the way, Evie, I'm trying to stay out of his reach, too. You might just mention to Dubay—"

"He hasn't seen you or heard from you. I'll tell him," agreed Evie. "Oh, Paul, nobody can save us now!"

"Then I guess we'll have to save ourselves," Paul said. After he had hung up, he stared at the doodle on the pad before him. It reflected his situation perfectly—he was sitting on a volcano here. Every time he went out, he took the risk he might run into his father. And Richard would stop at nothing to wrest the gold from his hands. If he had any sense, he'd jump in the Jaguar and head out to open country. So why didn't he?

He took his wallet out and flipped to the picture of Ari and him that he had found in Verena's apartment. Ever since he had found it, he couldn't stop taking it out and gazing at it. His heart lurched inside him. Ari! Where was she?

Ari had scrubbed at the chalice until it was gleaming, but she hadn't been able to get it to work again. She wondered if it transmitted only when they happened to be thinking of each other. She was about to give up when suddenly an image appeared. She gasped. It wasn't a three-dimensional image like the first one; it was as flat as if it were projected on a movie screen. Ari stared at it in amazement. There were two faces—her and Paul together! She was wearing a black dress, and suddenly she remembered that this was the photograph her mother had used for a Christmas card. That had been two years ago! Disappointment swept over her. She must be seeing projections of her own mind. This was an image from the past.

Just then she heard Rab's key in the lock. She quickly hid the chalice under a stack of underwear and shut the drawer.

Rab tossed his books on the kitchen table. "I've got it all set up for you to go talk to the police."

"Wonderful," said Ari in a hollow voice.

He cocked his head. "How are things going at school?"

"Pretty much the way you'd expect." She was surprised at how much the little things about the new school bothered her—the confusion of not knowing where her classes were, the warm water in the drinking fountains. The worst part was her recurring sensation that she recognized old classmates—when a closer look showed there were no familiar faces around her. Only the faces of strangers.

She had been there a week. At lunch she always sat alone in the big noisy cafeteria. But today a boy had sat down across from her and tried to make conversation.

"Hi," he had said. "You're new, aren't you? Where'd you go to school before?"

"St. Anselm's."

"Expensive school. Hard, too. Did you like it?"

She had nodded and her throat had clogged suddenly so she couldn't speak. She'd had friends there, real friends.

"I used to know a guy who went there—met him at a math competition. Cos Cosgrove. Did you know him?"

Ari's eyes had filled with tears.

"Did I say something wrong?" the boy had asked.

"N-no," she'd stuttered, dabbing at her eyes. "It's just that Cos was . . . a friend of mine, and I guess I'm sort of missing him."

"Yeah, he's great." The boy had chuckled. "He used to write to me, but I haven't heard from him in a long time. I'm bad about answering letters. What did you say your name was? I'll have to tell him that I ran into you."

"Anastasia Krupnik," Ari had answered promptly.

"Small world, isn't it?"

Too small, Ari had thought. Telling the boy that she had gone to St. Anselm's had been a dangerous blunder.

After that she could not shake the feeling that Cos was about to come around the corner any minute and throw his arms around her. It had made for a bad afternoon.

That night, Paul walked softly behind a lone woman on a dark, tree-lined street. A soft breeze blew, and bare branches moved with uneasy creaks of wood on wood. The woman in front of him quickened her step. Her heels made a sharp clicking sound on the pavement.

Paul picked up a stone and hurled it at a streetlamp. The glass globe exploded, instantly blanketing the sidewalk in darkness. The woman spun around. He ran at her and leapt on her like a cat. She fell under his weight, and his eyes glowed hot, his blood racing in excitement. He bent his head close to hers. Suddenly he stopped. His jaw fell open.

"Sophie!" he cried.

Sophie's ice-blue eyes glowed in the darkness. "It's too late to kill me, Paul," she whispered. "I'm already dead."

Paul's hands trembled as he helped her up off the sidewalk.

Sophie brushed herself off and eyed him hesitantly. "It's good to see you."

He was badly shaken. He realized he still wanted her, even after all that had happened between them. He wished with all his might he could erase the painful knowledge of her closeness to his father and gather her into his arms that minute. Instead he pushed his trembling hands into his pockets. "Yeah," he said. "Well . . ."

"I had to move out of my apartment," Sophie said. "Richard came there looking for you. He was certain he'd find us together."

Paul laughed bitterly.

"I never spied on you for him, Paul. You were wrong about that. I never did. I hate him."

Paul could hear the venom dripping from Sophie's words, and he believed her. But he hated Verena, too, and yet in some undefinable way they were close. He was afraid it was that way with Sophie and his father. "I wish neither of us had ever heard of my dad," he said, looking down at his sneakers. "I wish we could go back the way we were."

"We can! We'll hide from him. Just the two of us."

Paul put his arms around her and drew her close.

"Please," she said huskily. "Come home with me tonight."

Without saying another word they began walking together. Paul was afraid to speak for fear his doubts might spill out and break the frail connection that had formed between them. The strange thing was that he was certain that he would have gone with her even if she had been leading him to his doom.

In only a matter of minutes they stood before an apartment building that faced the grounds of St. Anselm's. The lights in the dusky stone buildings were burning low, and the campus trees and lawns were obscured in shadow.

"I used to go to school there," Paul told her. "See that big building over there by the trees? My locker for track was in there when I ran cross-country." A painful lump rose in his throat when he thought of how he and Ari had come to school together. "It seems like a long time ago," he said gruffly.

"I know," Sophie said. "I remember when I couldn't wait to graduate from high school. I didn't know when I was well-off. In those days the thing that scared me most was an algebra test."

That was before she'd met his father, of course. Paul was doing his best to blot out his knowledge that it was his father who had made Sophie into a vampire, but it was hard. Very hard.

They rode up in the elevator in silence. She opened the apartment door and turned on the light. "This place is kind of expensive, but I picked it because it has good solid doors." After they stepped inside, she slipped the deadbolt back into place.

Paul saw the lights of the city sparkling through the window. Nice view. But the furnishings were very simple. A carnation sat in a cola bottle on a coffee table. Why had she never taken him back to her place before?

Sophie sat down and the lamp beside the couch spotlighted her delicate features. He loved her slightly flared nostrils and sensitive, pale lips.

"You never let me come to your place before," he said.

"I needed to have a place that was completely private," she said. "A quiet place where I could be safe."

"So what's different all of a sudden? Why did you let me come here now?"

"I'm afraid, Paul." She pressed her hand to her mouth and looked at him with wide eyes. "I think Richard may have gone crazy."

"I think maybe he was always crazy." Paul's lips twisted wryly. He realized now why he had hung around Washington. Some part of him must have been hoping all along that he would run into Sophie. Ari, too, of course. How could he leave town when everyone he cared about was here? He laughed.

Sophie regarded him with puzzlement. "What are you laughing about?"

"Oh, I don't know." Paul shook his head. "It's

just that I'm so stupid, and I can't seem to help myself."

"Does Ari know where you are now?" she asked.

Paul shook his head.

"Richard seems to think he can find her and make her tell him where you're hiding," said Sophie. "You ought to warn her not to talk to him."

Paul fell to the couch. "I don't know where she is," he said flatly.

"Do you think Richard will find her? He's really acting weird, Paul. I think he might hurt her."

Paul thought about it. "I don't know. I guess whether he can find her will depend on how much she doesn't want to be found."

Far from the apartment, a single light burned in a dark office building. The letters on the glass office door read, "Angus Innes, Private Detective."

Detective Innes sat at the only desk. A haze of stagnant smoke hung in the room and a half-eaten candy bar sat by the typewriter. He was laboring over a report. "Followed subject to Budget-time Motel," he typed with two fingers. The phone rang. "Innes," he barked into the receiver.

"I'm trying to locate my daughter," said a soft voice. "Expense is no object."

Innes brightened. He liked the sound of the

case already. Immediately he reached for a pad and began taking notes. When he had finished, he had only a half-page of information on the subject, one Ari Montclair. He was not surprised the information he was given was so meager. Oftentimes husbands asking him to trace wives couldn't even give the color of their eyes. You had to wonder about the last time they looked. "Is she driving a car?" he asked. Cars were easier to trace than people. "Mazda registered under the name Gabrielle Montclair," he jotted on his notepad.

"I'll need some cash up front," he said after a moment. He didn't always ask for cash up front, but the customer's voice gave him the creeps. Somehow the guy made a simple finders job sound like an obscene phone call. Innes tucked the pencil behind one ear as he listened. "You'd be surprised how hard it is to hide these days," he assured the client. "Believe me, there are a hundred ways to track a runaway."

The detective hung up the phone and returned to his typing. He picked up his cigarette and took a deep drag. Good thing for him that families didn't get along. If there were no unfaithful spouses or runaway kids, he'd be out of business fast.

CHAPTER
SIX

SYBIL THREW HER ARMS AROUND COS'S NECK. "I'M
so glad you're still here! I was afraid you were
going to go to some other school and I wouldn't
have anybody to talk to."

Cos glanced around glumly at the uniformed
kids as they hurried past into the school buildings. "Yeah, well, my parents are giving me a
hard time. They keep talking about how things
are going to look on my college applications and
saying that I ought to stick it out."

Just then Jessie and Amanda passed by.
Amanda turned to smile at them.

"I wonder how murder would look on my
college applications," Cos muttered, watching
them.

"Don't talk that way." Sybil took his arm and
they began walking toward the Schuler Building.

"You know they were in that mob, Sybil.

They had to be. Doesn't it drive you crazy to see them looking so pleased with themselves?"

"Yes." Sybil lowered her voice. "But doesn't it make you feel better now that you know that Ari's okay?"

Knowing Ari was alive didn't make him feel as good as he would have thought. Was it better to be grieving because somebody was dead or to be feeling stupid because you were ditched for another guy? He wasn't sure. In some ways it almost amounted to the same thing.

"Cos!" someone called.

Cos turned and saw a petite blonde running to catch up with them, her book bag bouncing wildly. "Here," she said breathlessly, holding out an envelope. She gave a shy smile. "I thought you might want to have this."

Cos flipped it open. Ari's face stared back at him out of a glossy photo. His heart began pounding violently. She had been sitting in his lap in the big leather chair in the commons room. They had been caught by surprise by the yearbook photographer. They looked so happy, so carefree.

"Thanks," he mumbled.

The girl blushed and hurried off.

Cos stuffed the photograph inside a book. "I wonder who's kissing her now?" he said savagely.

"Cos!" cried Sybil.

He winced. "Sorry. I don't know what happened to the nice, easygoing guy I used to be. I don't even like myself anymore."

"When you love somebody," said Sybil, "all you should want is for them to be happy."

Cos surveyed her dismally. "I don't think you've ever been in love."

That afternoon Cos decided to stay late and help Mr. Simmons, his science teacher, organize the old chemicals in the chemistry lab's storeroom. He had been staying late after school almost every day this week. He still wasn't sure why he was doing it—he used to count every second until the final bell rang.

Maybe he just didn't want to be alone.

"I don't know how we ended up with all this junk," complained Mr. Simmons. "Some teachers can't stand to throw anything away—I understand that. But a fifteen-pound bag of baking soda?"

Cos knew he was supposed to say, "Throw it away," so Mr. Simmons could say, "Oh, I couldn't bear to." Mr. Simmons liked little jokes like this. But somehow this afternoon Cos couldn't bring himself to play the straight man. He shoved the bag of soda back under the shelf with his foot.

"I know this is a tough time for you, Cos," said Mr. Simmons.

Cos gazed at him in mute misery. Why *had* he volunteered to help clean the storeroom? He knew the answer now—because anything was better these days than dealing with his so-called friends. He hated the way they kept calling him at home and trying to cheer him up.

"It's a rough time for the entire school," said Mr. Simmons. "Four students dead." He shook his head. "No wonder everyone seems shell-shocked."

"You think they look shell-shocked?" said Cos bitterly. "I think they look pretty pleased with themselves." He slumped against the counter and pressed his hand against his temples. He felt a headache coming on. He never used to get headaches—until recently.

"Cos, I'm worried about you." Mr. Simmons's brow was deeply furrowed. "You know, it's no disgrace to ask for help. You ought to talk to somebody."

Cos gazed out the open door of the storage room. *He's right. I ought to talk to somebody. I want to talk to Ari. I'd just like to give her a piece of my mind, and then I'll feel better.*

"Promise me you'll do something about this depression," said Mr. Simmons.

"I will," he said. "I promise."

What he needed was to get hold of a Charlottesville phone book and find out Rab Barron's address.

That evening a knock sounded at the door of Sophie's apartment. For an instant Paul froze. Had Richard found them?

"Who is it?" his voice quavered.

"Delivery."

Paul sighed in relief as he unlocked the

62

deadbolt. He had been expecting this.

The delivery men carried the painted chest through the apartment door. "Put it in the bedroom," said Paul.

The men looked at him blankly. "Where?"

"In there." Paul indicated the open door to his and Sophie's room. But there was no bed in the room—which probably accounted for the men's confusion. Only a chest of drawers, a rocking chair, and a polished coffin, pushed discreetly over to the wall, where it was half hidden by the window draperies. The men clumsily dropped the painted sailor's chest to the floor.

When they had gone, Paul went down to the garage where his Jaguar was parked and began unloading the gold, which was still in black felt bags. After several trips he finally got all of it upstairs and into the sailor's chest.

Luckily Sophie wasn't around to see him. To his surprise it turned out she had a job working as a waitress at an all-night café. Good tips and flexible hours. He didn't mind. He was glad of the time alone so that he could store the gold in a safe place. Closing the bedroom door, he knelt by the chest and took out a golden chalice. His eyes lit up as he gazed at the design etched into the gold: a falcon seizing a duck. The chalice celebrated the victory of predators—no wonder his ancestors had stolen it. Paul rubbed his thumb lovingly over the design and gasped as a shimmering image appeared before him. "Ari!" he cried. The image of his twin's face obscured the sheen of gold. Ari's lips moved and a half-second later, he heard her words. "Paul? Are you alive?"

"I'm fine!" he cried loudly.

Her image was shifting and ill-defined. Her cheeks, her nose, her chin—everything looked tantalizingly close, but when he tried to touch her, his hand went right through her image, and his fingertips touched metal.

"Is it you, Ari?" he asked. "Is it really you? Or am I going crazy?"

She burst into laughter. "I can hear you. I can see you! Can you hear and see me?"

"Yes!" he cried breathlessly. Her words came a fraction of a second after her mouth moved. It was strange—as if he were getting the signal from far off somehow. When they were kids, Paul remembered, they had tried to make a telephone out of tin cans and a long string. This felt as shaky and unreliable as that. Every second he was afraid he would lose her. "Where are you, Ari? I'm not living with Dad anymore. I've moved in with Sophie."

"Sophie?" Her dark brows lifted in puzzlement. "Is that what you said?"

"So-phie," Paul repeated slowly.

"What happened to our father?" she asked.

"I'm hiding from him. He's bad."

"Maybe he stole the gold!" Ari cried. "Paul, I went back to the house, and the gold was gone. All that was left was this one chalice I found, the one I'm holding now. Paul? Can you hear me? Paul?"

Her image faded. Paul stared at his golden chalice for several minutes. He hadn't wanted to answer her, and as if in response to his hesitation, they had lost communication.

She was gone.

Cos's car sped through the night on the highway toward Charlottesville. He glanced at the scrap of paper lying on the seat beside him. As soon as he had copied down Rab's address, he had left. He knew he had to have it out with Ari as soon as possible.

He stopped at a service station and picked up a map of the town. Minutes later he was pulling into the apartment complex where Ari and Rab were living. The heat of his anger had kept him pressing hard on the accelerator all the way to Central Virginia, but now that he was driving into the dark parking lot, he was suddenly overcome by the embarrassed sensation that he was acting stupid.

The apartment complex was vast, and the phone book had not given an apartment number. He had no idea how to begin looking for her. Had he made a terrible mistake? Being here, staring at the anonymous square buildings that skirted the parking lot, made the betrayal seem that much more real. He felt vaguely sick. But just then a Mazda drove in and parked under a light at the other end of the lot. Even with the paint job, it looked familiar. Without hesitation he bolted from his car and sprinted toward the girl emerging from the driver's-side door.

"Ari!" he shouted. "Wait up!"

She stood frozen as he ran up beside her. "Cos?" she said weakly, her eyes wide.

"Is that all you can say?" he panted. "You let me think you're dead, you leave town without so much as a call, and that's all you can say?" His voice shook with anger.

A man coming downstairs gazed at them curiously.

"We can't talk here," Ari said, taking out her keys and glancing around furtively. "Come on upstairs."

"Where's Rab?" asked Cos, suddenly unsure that he wanted to go upstairs.

"Rab's at the library. He won't bother us."

A matter of opinion, thought Cos. Rab was bothering him already. But he followed Ari upstairs and into the apartment. As soon as they stepped inside, the bedroom door swung open and Rab stepped out, blinking in surprise. He was tall and skinny, with a hooked nose, a prominent Adam's apple, and black, V-shaped eyebrows. Cos couldn't understand what Ari saw in him—he really couldn't.

"I thought you were at the library," said Ari reproachfully.

"I got finished early," said Rab. He glanced at Cos and added, "But, hey, if you guys want to be alone, I'm out of here." He snatched a heavy book off the bed and fled.

When the door closed behind him, Cos exploded. "Jeez, Ari!"

"I thought he was at the library," she said.

"This is not about Rab," snapped Cos, though he wasn't so sure of his words. "This is about how you let me think you were dead. Was it too much trouble to give me a call just to let me know you got out of that fire alive? Do you have any idea what I went through? I was half out of my mind—not sleeping, not eating, flunking math tests right and left. Forget that I used to think I was in love with you and that you used to act like you felt the same way about me—never mind about all that. Just give a little thought to the sort of consideration that any decent person gives to any other human being on this planet!"

"I wanted to let you know I was alive," cried Ari. "I saw you were at Sybil's house the other night, and it was all I could do to keep from running up and ringing the doorbell."

Cos's fists clenched. "I bet," he muttered.

"I promised Rab I wouldn't tell anybody that I was still alive!" Ari cried. "It wasn't safe!"

"Rab told Sybil you were alive, though, didn't he?"

"He did?" Ari looked surprised.

"How do you think I found you? I guess Rab cared more about how Sybil felt than you cared about me."

Ari's eyes were glistening with tears. "Cos, I'm sorry," she whispered.

"It's kind of too late for that, isn't it?" said Cos, feeling sick to his stomach. "Way too late."

He turned and left without saying another word.

CHAPTER
SEVEN

DETECTIVE INNES RIPPED THE REPORT OUT OF THE typewriter and glanced at the clock. His client should be showing up any minute with the rest of the fee. He'd had no problem at all tracing the girl's car. A new license plate for a car registered in the name of Gabrielle Montclair had been sent care of Rab Barron to Charlottesville, Virginia, and a visit to that address had satisfied him that a girl fitting the runaway's description was living there. Simple.

Of course, there was a certain amount of showmanship involved in making the client feel he'd had his money's worth. Innes liked to mention "special confidential sources" and "my network of operatives." In reality, he was his only operative and his "special confidential sources" were records open to the public.

Since he was expecting a client, Innes had

left the office door unlocked, despite the late-ness of the hour. A dark shape loomed against the frosted glass of the door, and the door swung open.

Innes's smile froze on his face when his client stepped into the light. Richard Mont-clair's gleaming black hair was swept back theat-rically behind his ears, and his tightly stretched skin was as pallid as a corpse's. He was tall—but his black cape made him seem huge, larger than life. Some trick of the light made his eyes glow with a strange light.

Innes gulped. "I've got that report for you here."

Montclair smiled slightly as he pulled off his gloves. "Good," he said softly. "Here's the check." He laid it down on the desk.

Innes could feel the hair at the back of his neck bristling. Without saying a word he pushed the report across the desk.

Montclair picked it up and began to read it. His eyes seemed to glow hot and then dim. Innes became conscious of a trickle of sweat running down his spine. He groped at his sec-ond desk drawer and put his hand on the reas-suring butt of his pistol.

"This paragraph is not entirely clear," Mont-clair said softly. "Here, take a look." He edged around the desk.

Suddenly Innes panicked and pulled out the pistol. Montclair lunged at him. Innes heard the shot but saw only a flash of glittering eyes. Then a sharp hot pain and blackness enveloped him.

A few minutes later Richard stood up and wiped blood off his mouth with the back of his hand. He lifted his check off the desk, tore it up, and put the pieces in his pocket. "Expense is no object, naturally," he repeated softly. He folded Innes's report and stuffed it into his pocket, too. Stepping over the detective's body, he put his gloves back on and carefully went through the drawers and filing cabinets. At last he found a folder labeled "Montclair" and lifted out the evidence of the man's search for Ari.

Tucking the folder under his arm, he left and took the elevator down to the ground floor. The building was deserted. Stepping outside into the chill night, he gathered his cape around him. "Charlottesville, Virginia," he repeated softly. He got into the Mercedes parked at the curb outside.

He felt pleased with himself as he drove. It had been clever of him to trace Ari. When she realized what he had in mind, she would be afraid of him, of course, but that didn't bother him. He rather enjoyed the stark terror of his victims. Unlike his sister, he had never been squeamish about being a vampire.

Richard's heart grew cold at the thought of Gabrielle's death. Paul's carelessness had killed her. If it hadn't been for Paul, that mob would never have stormed Gabrielle's house. Now

Richard's nightmares were haunted by Gabrielle's face. In his dreams, her hair was on fire, and she was screaming for him to help her. She had always disappeared into flame before he could reach her.

His eyes narrowed. Paul had refused to listen to his advice—and he had refused to give him what was rightly his, whatever it was Gabrielle had been keeping for him. That left him no choice. He must drain the will out of Paul and make him the nerveless receptacle of his own wishes. A zombie, if you will. It was all he was fit for. Luckily Richard had an unusual knack for reducing vampires to that condition. He smiled. That was why he was so feared.

As for Ari, girls were more mature than boys. She was ready. And he could no longer risk the chance that she might come under some other vampire's influence. He had to make sure when she turned to the vampire life she was firmly yoked to him. Evie had gotten away from him, and now, for the time being, so had Paul. He couldn't let Ari slip from his grasp. He would bind her to him tightly with his blood.

Two hours later Richard was pulling into the apartment complex where Ari lived. He sneered. It was the sort of low-rent, confusing modern complex favored by college students. But after he was through with her, she wouldn't be living in such squalor anymore.

He climbed the stairs and hesitated a moment

outside the apartment, putting his ear to the door. It was silent. He slipped a credit card in the door and jiggled it. No luck. Glancing up and down the open hallway to make sure no one was coming, he drove his fist through the window. Broken glass crunched under his shoes as he reached in and pulled the window open. He took off his cape and let it fall to his feet. Then he lifted a long leg over the sill and awkwardly squeezed through the narrow opening. He could hear his pants ripping on the jagged glass and feel a sharp edge scraping his scalp, but in a minute or two he was inside.

Richard dusted the glass off his clothes and looked around. A white futon made up as a bed stood to his right and a tall reading lamp stood beside it. Now he would teach Ari what it meant to defy him, he thought. Maybe he would let her beg a little before he killed her. It would be good to let her feel her powerlessness. Remembering her face, it struck him suddenly how he loathed the skeptical, intelligent look in her eyes.

Leaving all the lights off, Richard searched the apartment until he found a broom. Then he stepped outside the front door, picked up his cape, and swept up the shattered glass. Only a few gleaming crumbs of glass remained on the hallway's cement floor when he silently stepped back into the dark apartment.

"What a great movie," Ari said. "I can't remember when I laughed so much."

Rab laughed as the two of them walked up the stairs. He had been willing to try anything to cheer her up after Cos had left. "We ought to do that kind of thing more often," he said. "We need to have some fun for a change. Do you like roller coasters?"

"No," she said. "A merry-go-round is as fast as I want to go." Suddenly she grabbed his arm. "Rab, something's wrong."

"You're a bundle of nerves, Ari. What could be wrong?" He had taken out his key to go inside. "You didn't hear anything, did you?"

"No, but I know something's wrong."

He hesitated. "I don't hear a thing."

Ari closed her eyes. "Listen with your heart, Rab. Listen hard."

Rab tried, but at first nothing came to him but a vague, crawling sense of unease. Then he saw a flutter of white. The curtain at the window was moving. He looked closer. The window had been shattered!

"Run, Ari!" he shouted. He was vaguely conscious of the sound of her steps disappearing down the cement hallway as the front door was flung open. A looming black shape stood in front of him. *His father!*

Rab backed away and reached in the broken window, jerking at the curtain. A piece of ragged cloth came off in his hand. His father's eyes bored into his. They were dark, yet luminous, like black coals threaded with a shifting, red fire.

"You gave me a ride one night," Richard said softly. "You know who I am. How?" The strange, glowing eyes narrowed. *"Who are you, Rab Barron?"*

Rab's hands trembled as he grabbed a lighter out of his pocket and touched the small flame to the swatch of curtain. The cloth was instantly ablaze.

Richard hissed and drew his cloak up over his mouth with one arm so that only his glittering eyes showed. Rab could feel flame licking at his fingers, but he didn't look down. The tall vampire backed away.

Shaking his burned fingers, Rab dropped the makeshift torch and darted into the safety of the apartment. He slammed the door and locked it, his breath coming in sharp gasps. Cold air streamed into the darkened apartment from the broken window, and Rab's teeth chattered. He was suddenly conscious of the stupidity of coming back in here. Now he was trapped. Richard had climbed in the broken window once. What was to stop him from climbing in again?

"Rab?" He heard Ari's faint voice. A tentative knocking sounded at the door. "Rab, are you all right?"

Rab opened it. "Ari! I told you to get away!" His eyes nervously scanned the hallway.

"I know!" She shivered. "I was halfway out of the parking lot before I realized I couldn't leave you. I just couldn't! I kept wondering what was happening. So I came back."

Rab yanked her inside and pulled the door shut. "He's gone. Somehow I scared him off. Maybe it was the fire. I saw him, Ari. It was Richard. He wasn't three feet away from me."

"But how did he find us?" she cried.

"I don't know, but he knows my name. You should have heard him—'Rab Barron,' he said, *'Who are you?'*"

"Oh, no," Ari whispered.

Rab felt a chill go up his spine. "What if he figures out who I am? I'll never forgive myself if something happens to Sybil because I've gotten myself mixed up in this." He rubbed his hands together, wincing. "We go to a motel for the rest of the night. First thing in the morning, I'm calling some movers. We're getting out of here."

"If he doesn't get us here, he'll get us someplace else." Her eyes were wide with terror. "He's going to catch up with us one way or another, no matter what we do."

Richard was shaking with rage as he drove away. He still didn't understand exactly what had gone wrong. This was the second time that the same boy had, almost casually, derailed his plans. The other incident had happened the night Richard's Mercedes had broken down and he had been forced to hitch a ride. Rab had only taken him a short distance before he had ordered him out of the car. Richard had been so angry he would have killed him then if he could have, but the boy had been brandishing a lighted cigarette, which had made it difficult. And tonight he had set a fire and waved it in Richard's face. Who was Rab Barron? Why did he keep turning up in such peculiarly unpleasant ways?

Richard drummed his pale fingers restlessly on the steering wheel. He saw a trend he didn't like—Evie had escaped, then Paul, and now Ari. Momentary setbacks, but annoying.

He decided right then he would take care of Evie first. More and more he had become convinced that Evie hadn't left Washington. All he needed to do was track her down. Ari could wait—until she was alone.

He *had* been under a lot of strain since Gabrielle's death, he reminded himself. He needed the magic she had once promised him. The magic cure, the treasure—whatever it was. It would give him new strength—he was sure of it. Paul had it, and Paul had to be staying with Sophie. He was sure of that, too. *Sophie.* He needed her to lead him to his son.

CHAPTER
EIGHT

THE NEXT EVENING, MINUTES AFTER SOPHIE LEFT for work, the doorbell rang. Paul wasn't particularly surprised—she often forgot her key. He sighed and opened the door thoughtlessly.

"Oh no!" he screamed.

The dark figure of his father stood before him, his eyes glittering with rage. In an instant Paul felt his father's cold fingers at the base of his neck and an electric current coursed through his veins. At once his body went numb and flabby. He couldn't move his eyes, and his limbs felt as if they belonged to someone else.

"Paul, my child," Richard said. "Where have you put Gabrielle's treasure?"

Paul closed his eyes. It was easy to remain silent because even keeping his eyes open was an effort. He felt a sudden sting of pain as his head snapped forward.

"Open your eyes!" snarled his father. "Answer me! Where is it?"

In spite of his fear, a faint glow of satisfaction burned deep in Paul's heart at the knowledge he could resist his father by refusing to speak. He felt the strain in his neck muscles as his head snapped back and forth. At last, reluctantly he opened his eyes to see his father's face inches from his own. "You think you're so smart," snarled Richard, shaking him again. "You think you can hold out on me, do you? Well, I can control every breath you take, every thought you think. I *will* find what you stole from me."

Paul stepped out of the apartment ahead of his father, mildly surprised that he was walking. His legs moved as if he were a windup toy; he seemed to have nothing to do with their odd halting motion. Richard did not close the apartment door behind them. Paul envisioned the fear and dismay that would cross Sophie's face when she would come home to find him missing and the apartment door wide open. His heart squeezed with pain. But he was powerless to do anything about it.

He was very tired, but it was a strange tiredness—more a lack of feeling and a lack of will than normal physical fatigue. It felt rather like an almost lethal dose of anesthetic. His feet kept propelling him through the streets of the city, his father silently trudging next to him. Why couldn't he resist? What was this power his father had?

At length he realized they were going up in the elevator to Evie's apartment. Once before, he remembered, his father had forced him to take this very same journey. He had felt the exact same way he did now. His life seemed to be a hopeless, turning wheel.

"You think you can refuse to tell me Gabrielle's secret," said Richard softly. "But you will soon find out how impossible it is for the mind to be free when the body is enslaved. You should never have tried to leave me."

A chill of fear made Paul shudder as the elevator jolted to a stop. The doors opened and his father shoved him ahead roughly. Paul's brain screamed for him to stop. This had all happened before—yet somehow he was helpless to prevent its happening again.

Only one thing was different. He blinked in surprise to see a brown paper package sitting in front of the door. His father bent to pick it up, holding it by its string so that he would not have to remove his hand from Paul's neck. The return address seemed to satisfy him, because he took it into the apartment and kicked the door shut.

Paul sat numbly on the long white couch while his father took the package into the kitchen. *This is my chance,* he told himself. *I should try to escape. He's not touching me. I'm free.* But it was all he could do, exerting his entire will, even to shift his gaze. What he saw then made his eyes open wide. A small diamond earring lay at his feet. Biting his lip with

81

the effort, Paul managed to nudge it under the couch with his shoe. Sweat beaded on his brow. His arms and legs were flabby, like rubber erasers. Confused thoughts whirled through his head. Evie. She had been back to the apartment! That was her earring. The brown paper package. Danger! He could hear the snip of scissors and the sound of his father whistling off-key in the kitchen.

Paul lunged off the couch. He reached for the doorknob with a groan. Utter panic flared in him powerfully, and he forced himself out the door and into the hall.

All of a sudden a deafening explosion lifted him off his feet and sent him tumbling. He landed flat on his stomach in smoke and darkness. Bits of plaster fell on his head. His ears were ringing painfully. Fear overwhelmed him and he crawled across the floor, desperate to escape. At last his fingers touched a closed door. To his relief, it was metal. The fire stairs. He staggered to his feet and jerked it open. A cool rush of air met him. He could hear screams and a distant siren as he groped his way downstairs.

At last he spotted the red of an exit light and lurched out into the night. From the sidewalk, he could see that smoke was pouring out of the apartment's shattered windows overhead. A fire truck had already arrived, and curious spectators were gathering on the sidewalk. "Maybe a gas main exploded," said somebody.

"It could be a bomb," said another voice. "Terrorists."

Paul smelled the faint scent of lemons and realized that someone was plucking at his shirt. "Paul!" Evie cried. Her startling lavender eyes brimmed with tears. She wore a mink coat and a broad diamond choker. "I had to do it," she whispered. "Did you see him? Is he dead yet? Tell me he's dead. He must be. You don't blame me, do you, Paul? He was going to kill me. You know he was."

Paul stared at her in numb shock.

Nearby firemen were pulling hoses off the truck. Clumps of people stood in pajamas and nightgowns, some with blankets wrapped around their shoulders.

"Let's get out of here!" he said. He pulled Evie away.

When they were out of sight of the firefighters, he sighed with relief. All he needed was for Evie to blurt out a confession in front of someone official. He took her pale hand in his. "Calm down," he said. "I don't blame you. But you can't talk about this, understand?"

"Dubay was in the bomb squad in the army," she whispered. "He knows all about bombs. But he didn't know what I planned to do. I was on my own. You won't blame Dubay, will you?"

"I won't blame anybody," said Paul wearily. "Get ahold of yourself, Evie."

She stared earnestly into his eyes. "You do think he's dead, don't you? It was an incendiary bomb. He certainly ought to be dead."

Paul licked his lips. She had darned near destroyed him as well. "He's gone," said Paul firmly. "The bomb was enough to knock me right off my feet, and I wasn't even inside the apartment. Smoke was pouring out of the place when I crawled away."

"It's very hard to kill a vampire," she whispered. "I had to be sure I made it powerful enough."

Paul shook his head. "Well, I hope you don't ever get mad at me, that's all."

Sophie! Suddenly he turned and bolted down the street.

"Paul, wait!" Evie cried. "Don't leave me . . ."

Within minutes he was back at the apartment. The front door was ajar just as his father had left it. Paul went in and looked around, mildly surprised that nothing had changed. How much time had passed since he'd left here? An hour perhaps? His father was gone—but he felt a curious flatness about Richard's abrupt death. Perhaps it hadn't registered yet. It seemed strange, almost comical, that his father's life had ended in a domestic quarrel. Paul was sure that when his father was threatening Evie, it had never occurred to him that she would kill him first.

Several hours later he heard the key in the lock. Sophie breezed into the room, a smile on her face. "This guy at work made a pass at me," she babbled. "He caught me back by the dishwasher and tried to take my dark glasses off." She laid her keys on the coffee table. "I think he'll try it again, too. I bit into his neck and took some blood. He blacked out for a minute, but when he came to he didn't even remember that I had bitten him. He said his knees felt weak and he was dizzy. He thought it was great. I suppose he imagines I kissed him. He doesn't have a clue."

Paul stared at her. "Richard is dead," he said baldly.

Sophie's mouth fell open so that he could see her fangs. Suddenly he wanted to take her into his arms and feel under his fingertips the pulsing blood in her neck. A moan escaped him as he moved toward her.

"Did you kill him?" She looked frightened. "What's going on, Paul? Did you do it?"

"No, not me. Evie." Paul stopped suddenly. "Why?" he said hoarsely. "Do you care?"

"It just gives me such a weird feeling. Are you . . . sure he's dead?"

"Yes," he said curtly. "Of course I'm sure. It was an incendiary bomb. It nearly got me, too."

"Oh, Paul!" Sophie's eyes filled up with tears.

"Which one of us do you love, Sophie?" Paul spoke between clenched teeth. "Which one?" He grabbed her by the hair and jerked her head back, exposing the long white curve of her throat.

She whimpered softly. "Please, don't be like

Richard. Please don't. I can't bear it if you are."

He caught his breath sharply. "No!" he whispered. "I'm not. I won't be like him." He opened his mouth suddenly and sank his fangs into the smooth skin of her neck. A sigh escaped her, and he felt his heart pound in excitement. He bit into her flesh until he could hear that her breath was coming in quick pants, but he wanted to give her deeper pain—he wanted to make her scream his name. The two of them fell to the floor. A sunburst exploded in his head when he heard her ragged high shriek. Damp with her thin blood, he rolled over on his back.

"You do love me, don't you?" he whispered.

"Yes, Paul," she said, sobbing.

He stared into her beautiful eyes, wishing he could believe her.

CHAPTER
NINE

ARI WAS DREADING HER VISIT TO THE POLICE STA-
tion, but she knew she had to go through with it
because she needed Aunt Gabrielle's money.
She hadn't been back to Washington since she
had found the chalice. The cold, gray day reflected her mood.

For some reason the streets near the station
were choked with police cars. She slowed the
car and glanced around her. At the end of the
block she saw an apartment building, its top
floor streaked with smoke stains. Several of its
windows were black, their panes of glass missing. Uniformed officers were walking in and out
of the main entrance to the apartment building,
carrying cameras and black bags.

"Dead!" exclaimed a strange voice. It seemed
to come from the direction of the gutted building. Ari whirled around but saw no one. All the

car's windows were closed, and the soft hum of her car's heater was steady. *It's my imagination. No one said anything.*

Impulsively, she pulled over and double-parked near a corner vending stand. She bought a newspaper from the fat man in a dirty apron and quickly began scanning it. "It was a bomb," the vendor said. "Right across the street. The cops are there now." He jerked his head toward the building.

"Did you see it go off?" asked Ari.

"No," admitted the man. "It happened late last night. I had already closed up."

"Was anybody hurt?" asked Ari.

He shook his head. "I guess nobody was home. They tell me the cops came over here with body bags, but when they went through the place, they didn't find a thing. The story's on page three."

Ari hastily opened the paper and saw the small heading at once. "Incendiary bomb suspected, say police. Experts on scene."

"Hey, lady! You can't park here!" someone yelled.

Ari spun around to see a police officer tapping his finger on her hood.

She jumped in the car and tossed the newspaper onto the seat behind her. No bodies had been found, even though it had happened late at night when most people are home in bed. Had the bombed apartment truly been empty? Or had vampires lived there?

She needed to put vampires out of her mind before she went in to talk to the police. But the strange voice sounded again like a doleful bell in her head. *"Dead."*

Ari longed to get back to Charlottesville and try to get some answers out of the chalice. More and more she clung to it. She polished it energetically whenever she could get a moment alone, but she had not been able to bring herself to tell Rab about its existence.

What if the chalice is some kind of transmitter? Am I putting Rab in danger by keeping it hidden in the new apartment? Radio transmitters can be traced. Maybe it's the same with the chalice.

But even as these thoughts raced through her mind, Ari knew she couldn't bear to part with it. It was her only link to her twin.

A few minutes later she eased the car into an open space outside the police station. She bit her lip anxiously, trying not to think about vampires or the explosion in the apartment building she had just driven past. She knew she had to think clearly when she faced the police.

She was ushered into a small room where a uniformed officer sat at a desk. The officer stood up and shook hands with her. She noticed that a stenographer was quietly seated nearby. "I'm Officer Nilson," he said. He was a thin man with a gray mustache. The dark flesh under his eyes gave him a tired, almost sorrowful appearance. "I understand you have some information to share with us about a case of suspected arson," he said.

Ari knew that Sybil's dad had spoken to the police on her behalf and she was glad. She felt as if the officer was looking at her respectfully, seeing her as the innocent victim of a crime. Maybe he also thought of her as the heiress of a substantial estate. It couldn't hurt.

"We appreciate your coming in today," he went on. "I understand that you've been traumatized by what happened."

"Yes," said Ari, sitting down and gripping the arms of the chair tightly. "I have."

It was harder than she had thought to go step-by-step over what had happened the night Aunt Gabrielle had died. Her eyes filled up with tears, and several times she had to pull tissues from the box beside her and blow her nose.

"You couldn't see who attacked your aunt?" prodded Officer Nilson.

"There were a lot of them," said Ari. "I could tell that much. But I was way up on the stairs where I couldn't really see what was happening. We had the old-fashioned kind of staircase with doors at the top and bottom. That is to say, the staircase is contained in a stair hall." By now she had almost persuaded herself that what she was saying was the truth, that she hadn't seen Gabrielle's attackers. "I was trying to keep my brother from going down," she added.

"Why was that?"

"I was afraid they would hurt him. I had heard somebody say, 'Go get him!'"

"Just put your mind back to that night," said Officer Nilson in a soothing voice, "and ask yourself if any of the voices you heard were familiar."

Ari shook her head. "All I could think about was protecting Paul. I never dreamed the mob would hurt Aunt Gabrielle. She was blocking their way. She was trying to keep them from going upstairs."

"And then?" he asked gently.

"I smelled kerosene," said Ari. "The door at the bottom of the stairs was open, and I could see the glow of something burning in front of Aunt Gabrielle—torches, I think—and then suddenly she was on fire!"

"Did she say anything? A name, perhaps? Did she call out to you?"

Ari shook her head. Looking back, she realized there had been something inhuman about the way Aunt Gabrielle had burned—the flames had leapt from her body as if she had been a candle and her blackened figure had grown thinner by the second. Ari hadn't seen what happened after she and Paul had turned and escaped, but she supposed Aunt Gabrielle had simply gone up in smoke. *The police found no bodies. Just like in the bombed building she had passed on the way here.*

Officer Nilson toyed with his pen. "Can you suggest any motive for this crime?"

"I think the only reason they killed Aunt Gabrielle was that she kept them from getting at Paul." Ari gulped. "Paul's girlfriend had been murdered a few weeks before, and I think they had worked themselves up to believing he had done it. He was the one they were trying to kill."

"By 'they,' you mean your brother's class-mates."

"Yes."

"So you recognized their voices," Nilson said, as if pouncing on an admission.

"Well, they sounded young," Ari said reluc-tantly. "And they knew Paul's name. Another thing—people at school had been looking at Paul so strangely that it was pretty clear what they were thinking. I guess that's why I jumped to the conclusion that it must have been our class-mates. It wasn't that I could recognize anybody's voice." She glanced up at him. "I was afraid to go back to school after that."

"I understand you're not living in the D.C. area now."

"No, I'm living in Virginia."

"With your brother?"

Ari hesitated. "No," she said. "Paul went to live with our father."

Officer Nilson lifted his pen expectantly. "And what is their present address?"

"I don't know."

"I understand you two are twins." He peered at her suspiciously. "You're telling me you don't know where he is?"

"My father and I don't get along," Ari said. "Our parents were divorced when we were born, and I didn't even meet my father until we moved up here when my mother died. Somehow Paul didn't feel the same way about him. That's why he went with our father, I suppose."

"He hasn't made any attempt to get in touch with you?" asked Officer Nilson skeptically.

Ari shrugged. "Everything's been such a mess since the fire. It's only now that I've started to straighten things out."

"And claim your aunt's estate," suggested the officer.

Ari felt herself go hot. *Was he hinting that she had killed Aunt Gabrielle herself for the money?* She licked her lips and shot him a quick, uncertain glance. The expression on the officer's face was bland, inoffensive. She realized she had to quit imagining that the police were after her. Her father was after her—and that was bad enough.

Officer Nilson had other questions, but after that none of them really claimed her attention. Ari was glad when at last she could sign her typed statement. As far as getting Aunt Gabrielle's estate settled, she had done all she could do. She stood up to leave.

"We may have further questions later," Officer Nilson said.

"Of course," said Ari faintly.

Thin winter sunshine met her when she stepped outside the police station. The sky had cleared, and the deep blue overhead was vaguely reassuring. Ari stood still a moment, blinking in the light. A sudden blast of a car horn made her jump. She darted her eyes toward the street and saw Sybil waving at her.

"Syb!" she cried, running down to the curb.

"Get in." Sybil smiled. "I just got my license."

Ari slid in on the other side. "How did you know I'd be here today?"

"I picked up the extension when Dad was talking to the cops," said Sybil, looking smug. She shot a glance at Ari. "It is okay that I surprised you like this, isn't it?"

"It's great!" Ari's face fell suddenly. "I don't suppose you've talked to Cos."

"I'm sorry, Ari." Sybil's words rushed out. "I let it out to Cos that you were staying with Rab, but I never figured he would actually go find you and yell at you. Rab was mad at me, but honestly it wasn't completely my fault. Cos took one look at me, and before I knew it, he had pretty much guessed everything I was trying so hard to keep secret."

"I hope nobody else finds out where I am."

"Believe me—I've been careful to keep my mouth shut. After the way I blew it with Cos, I've been petrified I'll give it away, so I just try not to bring your name up. I'm no good at secrets." She looked at Ari sadly. "I'm so sorry about your aunt. I guess the police were asking you who did it."

Ari nodded. "Yeah—but I was no help. I

couldn't see much of what happened."

Sybil tore ahead with a roar, and a huge bus veered sharply to avoid her. "Road hog," she muttered over the roar of its horn. "Well, look, there's no sense in us making ourselves miserable thinking about sad things. We've only got a little while together. Let's go get a sundae and do some catching up. I bet we can find someplace where we won't run into anybody we know."

Ari glanced at the car window. People on the sidewalk were gathering their coats tightly around them, their noses pink from the cold. Nobody but Sybil would even think of having a sundae on a day like this. She grinned. "Sounds perfect, Syb."

Sybil drove toward the monuments downtown and parked a block from the Air and Space Museum. Ari could hardly get a word in—but she didn't mind. Her friend's voice washed over her with the frivolous gossip, reminding her of how her life used to be. The chemistry teacher had been seen at a movie with the social studies teacher; a new student had been caught growing marijuana under lights in the chem lab storeroom. Even more interesting, rumor had it that Amanda was interested in Jessie.

"I don't see how she can be," cried Sybil. "I mean, I saw him in the library the other day reading up on medieval torture. Is that kinky or what?" She shrugged. "Honestly, Ari, it's totally gruesome at school without you. I don't have anybody that I can really talk to anymore."

She and Ari found a table at the Smithsonian's version of an old-fashioned ice cream parlor. Sybil dug into a banana split. "And Cos has lost his sense of humor," she went on. "He's no fun anymore."

"I guess I'm not much fun anymore either," Ari mumbled.

"Don't be silly. It's great seeing you." Sybil lifted the cherry off the whipped cream, her voice elaborately casual. "What do you hear from Paul?"

"Not much," said Ari. *Just the messages I get through the chalice, but I can't exactly tell you that.* "You've got to promise me you won't tell *anybody* where I am, Sybil."

Sybil crossed her heart and made a locking motion over her lips. "Never fear. Besides, I couldn't if I wanted to. After I spilled the beans to Cos, Rab wouldn't even give me his address or phone number. He says 'Don't call me. I'll call you.'" She wrapped a strand of carroty hair around her finger. "I'm giving some serious thought to straightening my hair. What do you think?"

Ari reached for her hand. "Don't change a thing about yourself, Syb," she said earnestly. "You're perfect."

Sybil drew back. "I wish you wouldn't say things like that, Ari. It sounds creepy, like those people who give trips to Disneyland to kids with incurable diseases."

Ari laughed. "Sorry. But honestly, I don't see why you're always worrying about how you look. You look great! Just like yourself!"

"I'd rather look like you," said Sybil frankly. "Or Cindy Crawford. I would straighten my hair in a minute except I'm afraid it'll look weird when it's growing out. You know—sort of half kinky and half straight. And I hear if you keep touching it up again and again at the roots, it can break off! I could end up bald!"

"Unlikely," said Ari, spooning up some ice cream. "What you need to decide is do you want to straighten it or don't you?"

"I'm not sure." Sybil regarded her spoon gloomily.

Ari shrugged. "I like it the way it is. It's different, distinctive. But it's no big deal. Whatever you do, it will grow out." Sybil's worries seemed completely incomprehensible. *It isn't quite the same as when you want to see your brother, but you're afraid if you do he will murder you.*

When they had finished the banana split, Ari reluctantly stood up. "I guess I'd better shove off."

"Already?"

"I don't want Rab to worry about me."

Sybil made a face. "Right. Well, I guess you'd better shove off, then. He's mad enough at me already."

When Ari was driving back to Virginia, she tried to count her blessings. But that only made her feel more sad. She was lucky that Rab had taken her in, lucky to have seen Sybil, lucky that she had her health. But somehow she could not feel at all lucky. The sky had turned the deep purple of dusk. Car headlights burned on the darkening highway, and the gray road seemed to stretch endlessly ahead of her. The brief visit with Sybil had only made her realize how very lonely she was.

CHAPTER
TEN

LATE THAT NIGHT, WHEN ARI WAS SURE RAB HAD gone to bed, she took out the chalice and polished it. She felt a sudden clutch of excitement when Paul's image formed in the air before her. "Paul!" she cried. "Is it you?"

"Ari!" His voice was whispery. "I've been trying to get through to you for hours. Richard is dead!"

Ari was so startled she dropped the chalice. It rolled around in a circle beside the futon. Paul's image had vanished. Frantically she snatched it up and rubbed it. To her relief Paul's image ballooned before the cup, wavy at first but then becoming clearer. His lips were moving, but she couldn't hear what he was saying. His curls were like black flames around his head.

"Paul! Paul!" Ari sobbed. "I can't hear you."

"What happened?" said the familiar voice. The words came a fraction of a second after they formed on his lips. "Where are you? What's going on?"

Ari darted an anxious glance at Rab's closed bedroom door. "I dropped the chalice," she said in a low voice. "Are you sure our father's dead? This is important, Paul. Are you sure?"

"I'm sure. It was some kind of incendiary bomb hidden in a parcel." Paul laughed harshly. "Boy, I bet he'd be surprised if he knew it was his girlfriend, Evie, that did it. He was always telling me that she was his puppet, that she didn't have a single thought of her own. Well, she fooled him. The bomb blew up in his face last night—"

"At the Brookridge Apartments," Ari finished.

"How did you know?" Paul's dark eyebrows rose in surprise. "Yeah, a fire gutted the place. We don't have to be afraid of him anymore. Do you realize what this means, Ari? We can be together again. You can come out of hiding." He spoke urgently. "Tell me where you are!" Suddenly his image vanished.

Rab's bedroom door opened. "Ari? What's going on?"

Ari stared at Rab as if he were a ghost. His uncombed hair stood out from his head, and he was wearing striped pajamas. "Nothing," she said. "I can't sleep." As Rab rubbed his eyes, she stealthily slid the chalice under the covers.

"I thought I heard voices," he said.

Ari shrugged, thankful that the chalice had gone silent. Her heart was pounding so violently she felt sick.

Rab walked to the front window, pushed the curtain aside, and looked out, frowning. "Could I have been dreaming? Could it have been somebody's television? Did you hear anything?"

She shook her head, afraid to open her mouth. What if she spoke and the chalice suddenly answered her? She was afraid if Rab found out she had been using it to talk with her twin, he would insist she get rid of it.

Rab walked over to the kitchen. He opened the refrigerator door, poured a glass of milk, and gulped it down. "I've got to get some sleep," he said, putting the glass down on the counter. "The last couple of days I've been a wreck. If I keep going on like this, I'll go nuts. Richard scared the hell out of me. I keep thinking what if he gets to Sybil? I haven't even warned her. How *could* I warn her? Nothing I could tell her even makes any sense."

Richard couldn't hurt them anymore—but she couldn't tell Rab that. He would want to know how she had found out Richard was dead.

Rab shuffled back toward the bedroom. He hesitated in the doorway and looked at her. "Are you sure everything's okay? I'm having a funny feeling."

"I'm fine." Ari smiled. She yawned ostentatiously and snuggled down under the covers.

101

"Okay, then. Good night." Rab smiled as he closed the door.

After the ribbon of light under his door disappeared, Ari forced herself to count to a hundred. Then she counted again. Finally she whipped the chalice out from under the covers. It felt warm, as if electricity had been surging through it. She brushed it gently against her cheek. Its jewels caught the light that leaked in around the curtains. Ari was sick with longing for her twin. Yet he had startled her by his urgent demand to know where she was—and her courage had suddenly vanished. She had been so very afraid of him the night of the fire. Could she trust him now? *Was* everything different now that their father was dead?

Paul stared at the chalice, frowning. As soon as he had asked Ari where she was, her image had vanished. That could mean only one thing— she didn't want to tell him. She was afraid of him.

An icy desolation swept over his body.

He heard Sophie come in and quickly stashed the chalice in the chest. "Hi," he said. He forced himself to smile as he walked into the living room. "Is that guy at work still after you?"

"It's the funniest thing, Paul. He grabbed me around the waist tonight when I was putting the dishes away. He thinks we're working up to major passion, you know? So I put my arms around his neck, drew him real close, and dug my fangs in deep and got a good gulp. You should have seen him sag against the counter. I was afraid he was going to pass out on me, which *would* have been mess. I mean, people were bound to notice if he went down with a big thud. But luckily he didn't. He just sort of wilted and got this glassy-eyed look. I heard him telling somebody later that he didn't seem to have his old energy, and he thought he'd better start taking vitamins." She kicked off her shoes. "I'm going to have to be careful not to overdo it. I don't want to kill him."

"Why not?" asked Paul viciously. "I could really enjoy killing him."

"Goodness, Paul, it's not as if I *like* him or anything."

Sophie looked at him uneasily. "Is something wrong? You sound kind of—depressed."

"I guess I am," Paul admitted. "Let's get out of here. I'm going stir crazy."

Paul knew Sophie was staring at him as they walked to the car. He avoided her eyes. How could he tell her what was bothering him? He couldn't let on that he was in touch with Ari without letting on that he had the gold—and that was a secret he wasn't willing to share.

When they got to the car, Paul instinctively headed south on Wisconsin Avenue. He realized he was driving toward Georgetown. He was drawn to the old neighborhood as if it were a powerful magnet. Being there somehow made him feel closer to Ari. He edged the car into a parking place.

"Here?" asked Sophie, glancing over her shoulder at the entrance to the neon-lit bar that was spilling loud music out onto the street. "I thought you didn't like this place."

Paul shrugged. "I'm in the mood for noise." *Anything to drown out the truth: Ari is afraid of me.*

He and Sophie pushed their way through the crowd in the bar. The white faces of the bar patrons, pale men with chiseled cheekbones, skinny women with bony, jeweled hands and strange eyes made nightmarish vignettes in the darkness. Vampires, all of them. The bar was a notorious vampire hangout, but Paul found himself scanning the crowd anxiously nevertheless. Once he had run into Jessie and Ari's boyfriend here. It wasn't the kind of place where anybody checked IDs, which made it a draw for the occasional high school student who wasn't put off by the unusual-looking clientele.

A bald bartender with hollow eyes, cadaverously thin, placed a couple of Bloody Marys before them.

Paul caught a glimpse of two familiar-looking women. Both were very thin and both wore black. One had her hair slicked back so tightly it looked enameled to her skull. Her eyebrows were plucked to a thin line over deeply shadowed gray eyes. The other wore full, black crepe pants and had a thick fringe of blunt-cut

hair that fell over one eye. Gwendolyn and
Tippi, if he remembered right. Friends of Aunt
Gabrielle's. Paul vaguely recalled that one of
them was a graphic artist and the other was
some kind of dancer. He couldn't remember
who was who. Not that it particularly mattered.

The one with the pants met his stare and
strode toward him, tossing her hair out of her
eye. "You poor boy. I'm Gwendolyn, remember?
I can't tell you how sorry Tippi and I are about
dear, dear Gabrielle." Her voice was husky with
emotion.

Tippi touched a tissue to her eyes. "Tragic
loss," she murmured. "And terrifying. I've
scarcely slept a wink since it happened."

"I've had a lot of deaths in my family lately,"
said Paul, gulping down his drink. "I guess you
heard that my father died last night."

Gwendolyn's eyes were wary. "Were you and
Richard close?" she inquired.

Paul met her gaze unflinchingly. "Of course
not. There's no point in my being a hypocrite.
I'm glad he's dead. Isn't everybody?"

"I suppose he had his admirers." Tippi
glanced at Sophie.

Paul felt rage swelling in him. He squeezed
his eyes shut.

Sophie touched his shoulder. "Would you
like to dance, Paul?"

Without a word Paul slid off the bar stool
and took her into his arms. A flickering strobe

light cast a confusing glow around the crowded room. The music was so loud, Paul could feel its vibration in his fangs. Sophie's hair turned red in the odd light. Her eyes were as blue as a blue note, he thought, and just as sad. He could feel the soft movement of her rib cage as she breathed, the precious fragility of her body. "I love you," he said. "That's why I sometimes act so crazy."

She rested her head on his shoulder. "I love you, too."

"What do you think Tippi meant, looking at you that way?" he asked.

"Nothing!" she cried, glancing up at him in alarm. "She's only nervous and upset. Richard is dead, Paul. Don't let him ruin things for us now."

Paul closed his eyes and swallowed hard. She was right. He had to get ahold of himself. In his former life Ari had always been his safe port in the stormy sea of emotion—the one he could trust absolutely. Now she was gone. If he drove Sophie away as well, he would die of loneliness.

Paul felt someone touch his shoulder, and he spun around. It was Evie in a tight white dress, a diamond choker encircling her skinny neck. Dubay was with her. His muscles bulged under his black T-shirt; he looked more like Evie's bodyguard than her companion. A small gold stud gleamed in his nostril.

"Will you dance with me, Paul?" Evie asked.

Paul knew that if he danced with Evie that meant Dubay would dance with Sophie, but he didn't feel he had much of a choice. Evie's face was haggard, and she looked jumpy enough to cause a scene. Already he felt as if people were staring at them. "Sure," he said. "I expect Dubay and Sophie have a lot of old times to talk over." He could hear the acid in his own voice. Sophie glanced nervously over her shoulder as Dubay put his arm around her and whisked her away.

When Paul turned back to Evie, her eyes were swimming with tears. "Richard was a beautiful dancer," she said.

"Get a grip, Evie," Paul snapped. "If you'd given him a chance, he'd have killed you."

"I know." She gasped. "I did the only thing I could do. I have no regrets. None at all. Only, please, Paul, don't tell anybody what I did." Her feet moved mechanically as they danced.

"Nobody cares, Evie."

"Do you really think that?" Evie glanced over her shoulder nervously.

"Do you see anybody crying? I was afraid of him, and you were afraid of him too. And we were the ones he was *close* to. Lately I think everybody was afraid of him."

Evie placed her white hand confidingly on his chest. "I don't want anybody to know what I did, Paul. Not even Dubay. It would be awful if he were afraid of me."

He smiled. "I'll keep my mouth shut."

"I didn't want to hurt Richard," Evie went

107

on, as if she were talking to herself. "But I had to. I was crazy with fear. You know what he was like."

Paul glanced over at Sophie and Dubay, who were dancing rather stiffly. The bar was very crowded, so it was hard to move and they did not look as if they were enjoying themselves. Paul was glad.

"Sophie is such a nice girl," said Evie, following his gaze. "I've always thought so."

Paul swallowed. *Since when?* he thought. *Since my father made her?* "It's too crowded here to dance," he said gruffly. "Let's go find the others."

CHAPTER
ELEVEN

"WHAT'S WRONG, PAUL?" SOPHIE SPRAWLED ON THE couch when they got back to the apartment and gazed at him. "If you can't talk to me, how can we be close?"

"It's Ari," he said, burying his face in his hands. "We've been together our whole lives, and now I've lost her. I don't even know how to start looking for her."

"Maybe you could put an ad in the personals column," suggested Sophie.

"She may not even be in the city. Somehow I feel like she can't be too far away. But—I think she's hiding from me, Sophie." His voice cracked.

"You live in different worlds now." Sophie looked at him shyly. "Maybe it's something you need to get used to."

Paul leapt up abruptly. "I'm going out," he said.

"Paul!"

"I've got to be alone," he said, thrusting his hands in his pockets. "Don't worry," he said bitterly. "I'll come back. Where else would I go?"

The Jaguar seldom failed to comfort Paul. He loved its long hood, the hum of its powerful engine, and the leathery smell of the interior. But it could not lift his spirits tonight. He drove downtown toward the lighted monuments, feeling as if he were driving through a city of the dead. In a way, he was. His cold flesh and the inhuman crystalline gaze that met him in the rearview mirror told him that he was a vampire. But nothing brought the bitter truth home more than the corruption he smelled when he met others like him—the expensive clothes bought with money stripped from dead bodies, the lies, the hungry look. He remembered once seeing a list of the symptoms of death. "Corruption is an absolute sign of death," it had concluded. *Corruption—a rot of the soul. I live with corruption, among the dead. Sophie's the best part of it—but what can we give each other but pain?*

Too depressed to keep driving, Paul let the car glide to a stop. He glanced toward the lighted Capitol Building and was startled to see a girl wading in an ornate fountain. She was lifting her filmy skirt up with one hand and holding her shoes in the other. Silken blond hair fell to the shoulders of her skimpy gown. She laughed with wild abandon. She was a beautiful sight, and Paul's spirits lifted. The wet dress clung to her thighs and legs so that she looked like a pale but living statue. He realized that she had to be drunk. That water was crusted with ice, yet she was splashing around in it. She looked up suddenly and waved at him.

Paul felt his blood turn cold. "Verena!" he cried. He leapt out of his car.

Trailing streams of water, she came slowly toward him, her feet leaving blurred wet footprints on the sidewalk. She pushed the hair out of her eyes and grinned, a dimple teasing the corner of her mouth. "It's fate," she said. "Like a spider and a fly—you come to me every time. Don't you, love, huh?"

She drew close to him and rested her wet hand on the back of his neck. Water trickled down his back, and Paul felt a chill of apprehension. "I was out for a drive," he gulped. "Funny that I should run into you this way."

"You came by just in time." She grinned. "I need a ride."

"How'd you get here?" He glanced around. "Where's your car?"

"I hitchhiked," she said. "The Marine I came with is over there somewhere." She gestured vaguely. "In his old smelly Volkswagen."

"Is he dead?"

"Sure." She giggled, and Paul felt her fingernails raking through his hair. "I hate military haircuts, don't you? All that stubble and the yucky shiny scalp underneath. I'd much rather ride with you."

111

"You'll get my car wet."

"Don't worry. It'll dry." She got in the Jaguar and slid her strappy sandals onto her white feet.

Reluctantly Paul got in behind the wheel. He hoped Sophie didn't notice how wet the car had gotten. Despite himself, he laughed. "Verena, you're like poison ivy. I can't get rid of you."

"Liar. You *love* the way you keep running into me. Your little heart goes pit-a-pat whenever you see me. Admit it!"

Paul regarded her stonily.

"You know why you like me?" Verena went on. "It's because you don't have to pretend to be nicer when you're with me. You can let yourself go and be mean. I know you better than you know yourself, snooks. You can pull over right here," she said.

Paul thought she was going to get out, but instead of making a move to open the door she leaned toward him and rested her arm on the seat behind him. He was repelled by the synthetic smell of her perfume. "I notice you got yourself a car like mine," she cooed.

Paul felt a sliver of doubt pierce his heart. Was that why he had wanted the Jaguar? Because Verena had somehow planted the idea in him? "Verena, what happens when you make somebody into a vampire? I mean, what happens between you? I need to know."

"I dunno. There's something there, that's all. I don't think about it." She shook her wet hair negligently, and a spray of water hit him in the face.

"You *must* think about it," he said desperately. "You told me yourself about all the guys you had done it to."

"I have sort of a theory," she said, letting a fingernail slide down his cheek. "I'm not as stupid as you think, you know. I have ideas. I figure it's kind of like when ducklings hatch. The first thing they see they follow around, even if it's some guy with a beard who doesn't even look a bit like a mother duck. Weird, isn't it?" She threw her skinny arm around his neck, and he grew dizzy when he felt her breath tickling his cheek. "Lot of guys think I'm awfully attractive," she whispered. "That's how I've gotten so many, many pretty young boys."

"You're not attractive," said Paul harshly. "You're tacky and cheap." He was pleased when she drew back from him a little.

"I think I have class," she mumbled, obviously stung. "Besides, what do you care about how cheap I am? You can't get enough of me."

The vicious tone told him it was coming, yet the sudden pain staggered him. He felt the sickening feeling of his skin parting, and he looked down in horror to see a gash at the base of his neck. Blue veins pulsed in the trembling flesh as if he were a piece of meat. He could feel beads of sweat on his forehead, the strength leaking out of him. He saw her pink tongue curl out of her mouth and disappear into the wound. She

113

probed his flesh—then he heard her greedy slurp. Nausea rose in his throat as he saw she had pressed her lips tight to his skin. The suction was sickening, unbearable. "No, Verena," he whispered. "Stop! You're going to kill me."

"I *can't* kill you, dum-dum. But you hate me, don't you?" She stopped for a moment to speak, and to his relief he was able to catch his breath. She peered into his eyes, her face close to his. Her lips were flecked with the foam of his blood. "When you hate me, that makes it better," she said softly. "I love it when boys fight me. I always win."

Paul had a ghastly flash of recognition—as if it were his own cruelty he saw reflected in Verena's eyes. "I'm not like you," he protested weakly, writhing in her grip. "I'm not a bit like you."

Her laughter sounded in his ears. "Are you trying to tell me you aren't a vampire, Paul?" She giggled. "I know you are. I made you into one myself."

He felt her lips brush his skin, and then her teeth were hard against him again, digging into him. It was as if she were turning him inside out; he reeled with the sense he was coming apart, disintegrating. At last, mercifully, he blacked out.

When he came to, Verena's arms were locked around his neck and she was asleep, her head resting on his chest. Her cheek was sticky, and he realized with disgust that it was damp with his blood. Paul closed his eyes, wishing the smell of her perfume didn't make him sick. "When are you going to leave me alone?" he muttered.

She sat up and brushed her hair out of her face. "I like that! You're the one that's always coming on to me."

Paul clenched his fist, relieved to see that he could still do that much. "Get out." He pulled the door open and shoved her out onto the street. Suddenly he felt woozy. As he drove off, he could see that his car was weaving crazily down the empty street. And in the rearview mirror he could see her sitting on the pavement, her legs out before her. She was laughing.

Paul coughed. Her perfume clung to the car. He rolled down the windows and let the cold air whistle noisily through it. He understood her laughter now. A thread he could not see, as invisible and thin as a strand from a spider's web, somehow kept drawing him toward her. How comical his efforts to escape must seem to her. He didn't understand the hold she had on him; Verena didn't understand it herself. But he was dismally certain that she was as much a part of his life now as the color of his eyes.

He turned toward Georgetown and drove down the street where he used to live. If only he could go back in time, back to that distant past, before he and Ari had come here, before they had met their father—before the horror. But it was no use. Those days were gone.

It was late and the windows of the houses were dark. Gazing ahead, Paul could see the dark gap, like a missing tooth, where his aunt's house had been.

His fingers rested lightly on the steering wheel as he let the car roll slowly on the silent street. He stared at the heaps of bricks and stacks of burned wood by the sidewalk. The ruins of the house had been flattened, and little remained but the foundation. He could see the trees of the garden behind the house. Aunt Gabrielle's raised flower beds were heaped with torn insulation. The fireplace where he had found the treasure had been dismantled; its bricks lay in piles in front of the house. Someone had taken a wrecking ball to it. He thought of the ghosts that had once haunted the old house—the medieval vampire and her companion, the fanged cats. A vampire's diary had been in Aunt Gabrielle's library, the fabric worn off of its wooden cover, its bookplate stained with blood. Where were these ghosts from the past now? Had they been scoured from the earth by the holocaust that had consumed the house, just as Aunt Gabrielle had been?

Paul shivered. He was part of their world now, and just as vulnerable to flames. He glanced at the sign that stood before the ruined house—Rogers Construction Company—and made a mental note.

Driving home, Paul turned the demolition of the house over in his mind, wondering what to

116

make of it. He supposed the city had the power to order an unsafe structure torn down, but the speed at which the house had been leveled had made it look like a private job. Who was paying Rogers Construction Company?

When he got home, Paul crept guiltily into the apartment. He was glad to see that Sophie was not around. He stripped off his clothes and stuffed them into the washing machine, anxious to drown the stench of Verena's perfume in the soapy water.

After pacing the apartment for a few minutes, he snatched up the phone and dialed the number of Rogers Construction Company. Four rings later their answering machine came on. "Our regular office hours are Monday through Friday, eight-thirty to five. Please call again during our regular hours or leave a message after the beep."

Paul knew he would be sound asleep during their regular office hours, so he left a message. Who had employed them for a demolition job on N Street? he asked. He hung up and glanced at the clock. Six A.M. Where was Sophie? Dawn would be coming soon, and he felt the familiar prickle of uneasiness as the time approached for him to fold himself into the coffin. Maybe Rogers Construction would leave an answer on his voice mail tomorrow. It couldn't hurt to ask. The trail might lead him to Ari. And that was all he wanted.

The door opened and Sophie walked in. Paul

was absurdly glad to see her. "Hi! Where've you been?"

"Hunting," she said casually.

He could have guessed it. Her pale flesh pulsed with life, and at that instant she could have almost passed as human. She also smelled faintly of beer. She must have been feeding on drunks. If any smell of Verena's perfume lingered, he figured the smell of beer would cover it.

Sophie wrinkled her nose, which made his heart stop. What if Verena's perfume clung to his hair!

"Aren't you wearing different clothes than you were earlier?" she asked.

Paul felt himself go hot. "I decided to do some washing."

"I hope you remembered to use soap this time." Sophie's eyes laughed at him.

Paul stared at her guiltily. Wasn't there some line from *Macbeth* that went, "All the perfumes of Araby will not sweeten this little hand"? He felt as if he could never cleanse himself after touching Verena. How could he be angry at Sophie for what she had done with his father? He was drawn to Verena even though he loathed her. He seemed powerless to rid himself of her.

He touched the tip of Sophie's nose with his finger. "You always remind me of a flower," he said huskily. "Your eyes are blue like forget-me-nots."

She took his hand in hers and clutched it to

her breast. "You make me happy," she said simply. For that split second they seemed to Paul like any other ordinary couple. But then Sophie glanced uneasily at the clock. "Coffin time," she whispered.

Horror crawled like a slug up Paul's spine as he followed Sophie into the bedroom. He held back a little when she lay down in the casket.

"Come on!" she urged. "It's time."

With a shudder he lowered himself onto her. Every time the lid closed down, he was certain that this time he wouldn't be able to breathe. The coffin fell shut suddenly with a clunk, magnifying his despair.

"Ari!" he whispered into the stifling blackness. "Where are you?"

CHAPTER
TWELVE

AFTER SCHOOL, ARI STOPPED BY AN OPTICIAN'S OF-
fice. A pair of giant eyeglasses hung over the
door, almost a visual joke, but the office itself
was businesslike: a receptionist's desk and a
room containing many racks filled with eyeglass
frames. The walls were mirrored so that Ari saw
her anxious face reflected back at her a hundred
times.

"Are my lenses ready?" Ari asked. "My name
is Ari Montclair."

The receptionist was a middle-aged woman
with woolly hair. Her glasses hung on a chain
around her neck. "I've got them here." She
reached into a file. "I remember them particularly, because it was such an unusual order. We
had to special-order that lavender color, so
there's an added charge." She put the lens case
on the counter and watched as Ari wrote a

check. "We hardly ever get an order for nonprescription contact lenses," she went on.

Ari smiled noncommittally as she tore off the check.

The receptionist tucked the check into her cash drawer. "Well, I hope you enjoy them, dear. And I hope he's worth it."

Ari pocketed the lens case and hurried out, her ears burning. *She thinks I'm buying them to attract a boy.* It was stupid, but it made her think of Cos. Tears stung her eyes as she slipped into the Mazda and drove away.

Cos has lost his sense of humor, Sybil had said. The thought of Cos being hurt by her was almost more than Ari could bear. She wanted to see him, to touch him, to run her hands through his messy hair. The problem was, she thought sadly, he certainly didn't want to see her. He had made that very clear. And he had every right to be angry. What she had done to him was unforgivable. But she'd had no choice. . . .

Just then Ari saw what she was looking for: a sign that read, CUT 'N' CURL HAIR SALON. She parked hastily.

As she walked inside, she was met by the noise of blow dryers. The big room smelled of hair spray. Scraps of hair lay on the floor. "Are you my four o'clock?" a tall woman called cheerfully. "I'm Dianne."

Ari nodded and climbed into the chair. Dianne pumped up the chair until Ari's feet were off the floor. It gave her an odd, marooned feeling. *There's no going back now. I'm really going to do this,* she thought.

The woman lifted a strand of her black hair. "What exactly do you have in mind?" she asked.

"Cut it short," said Ari.

"How short? Do you want it layered or blunt cut, bangs or not, side part or middle part?"

"Quite short. I don't care about anything else."

"Do you want to see some pictures, to help you make up your mind?" asked the woman.

"Not really." Ari gazed at the big mirror. With the white apron tied under her chin, she looked as if she were being readied for the guillotine.

"When hair is long like this, I like to make sure people are really ready to go short," said the hairdresser. "I hate it when they burst into tears and scream that I've ruined them."

Ari looked at her incredulously. It would take more than short hair to make her burst into tears. People who cried about something like that must not have any idea what real trouble was. "You've got to be kidding," she said flatly. "I told you to cut it short. Now cut!"

The woman shrugged and began snipping. As the black curls piled up on the linoleum around the chair, Ari began to hope she hadn't made the woman angry. For the first time she began to sympathize with Sybil's fear of baldness.

"Say when," said Dianne.

Ari could feel cold air on the back of her

neck, and her ears felt chilled. Even more ominously, her entire head felt strangely light. "I think that's short enough," she said.

After evening Ari's hair with a pair of smaller scissors and a razor, Dianne held up a mirror. Ari blinked, scarcely able to recognize herself. For some reason her lack of hair made her look much thinner.

"Some people don't want to bother to have to comb it," said the woman, untying the big bib. She shook the bib out, and hair filled the air.

Coughing, Ari wrote her a check.

"It looks terrific," beamed Dianne. "You've got the looks for it. I hope you enjoy it."

Ari's next stop was a drugstore where she bought a tin of white baby powder and a makeup brush. Then she went into a boutique and bought a pair of black jeans and a black T-shirt. The saleswoman wrapped both items in sheets of tissue paper and stuffed them in a pink, shiny bag. "There you are!" she said brightly. "I hope you enjoy them."

Ari wished people would quit harping on enjoyment. It gave her a strange feeling, because enjoyment wasn't what she had in mind at all.

Paul rubbed his eyes, turned on the light, and picked up the phone. The staccato dial tone told him he had a message. He rapidly punched some numbers into the phone and listened as the message played. "This is Rogers Construction

Company returning your call," said a nasal voice. "The law firm of Cross, Thrimbell, and Thicket is employing us on the demolition job you mentioned. If you have any questions, you should address yourself directly to them."

Paul hung up and flipped rapidly through the phone book. When he dialed Cross, Thrimbell, and Thicket, he expected to get another answering machine—it was after five. But he had reckoned without considering the long working hours of law firms. "Cross, Thrimbell, and Thicket," said an unmistakably human voice. Paul could hear the click of keypunching in the background.

"I have a question about the demolition work you have arranged for Rogers Construction Company to do on N Street," he said.

"Mr. Higgins is in charge of that, I believe. He'll be in tomorrow. Is this Rogers Construction Company calling?"

"No," said Paul, thrown a little off balance. "I'm a concerned citizen."

"Oh. Well, if you have any questions or complaints you should address them to Mr. Higgins's attention at this office."

"All I want to know is who your client is!"

"I'm afraid that information is confidential," said the voice. A click severed the connection.

Paul threw the receiver, and the phone fell to the floor with a clang.

"What was that noise?" Sophie walked out of the bathroom, her hair still wet from the shower.

"I threw the phone," Paul mumbled. "I'm not having any luck tracing Ari."

"I'm sorry." She hesitated. "Paul, don't you think you'd better give up? Maybe this isn't meant to be."

"I'll never give up!" He clenched his fists. "I need my sister. You don't understand."

"I was hoping I would be enough for you," she said, her sad eyes meeting his.

"I can't explain." He buried his face in his hands. "It's like I'm cut off at the roots. I've got to have her. If I can find her, I'm going to fix it so that we'll never be apart again."

"How are you going to do that?" she asked.

He met her gaze steadily. "How do you think?"

Sophie gulped.

"You think I'm wrong, don't you?" he shouted. "You think I ought not to do it."

She shook her head. Her eyes were wide with fright. "I never said that, Paul. I'd better be going. I'll be late for work." She threw on a dress and slammed the door behind her.

Paul was so frustrated that he couldn't think straight. He went into the bedroom and took the chalice out of the chest, staring at it intently. Then he tried rubbing it. Nothing. He had polished it so much, he was afraid he might have worn it out. The chest was full of gold, gold he had never touched, gold he had no use for. He felt helpless as he sat staring at it. Slowly he picked up a gold plate. It had a heavy rim studded with jewels and engraved with an ornate design. Maybe he would have better luck with a different piece of gold. Paul began polishing it, and suddenly he heard people laughing. He looked around, then blinked rapidly as a faint blurred image appeared on the plate. His breath quickened with excitement as he felt the gold plate grow warm in his hands. On the flat part of the plate, framed by the jeweled rim, a girl was squirming and laughing. Her black hair was silhouetted against something brown, and there was someone with her who looked shorter and fairer.

Paul looked closely at the image as it cleared, and its colors became vivid. The other figure wasn't shorter, as Paul had thought; he was only sitting down. Ari was sitting in Cos's lap, and they were both laughing. Paul recognized where they were now—the commons room at St. Anselm's. He could just barely make out the fireplace beyond them. They were in the big leather chair in the commons room, and its back was so tall that passersby could not see them. That was probably why they were there—it was the perfect place for making out. Paul could see them clearly now and could hear the familiar dull clamor of kids changing classes in the hall behind them. Cos spoke clearly. "We can't go on meeting like this." His eyes narrowed in amusement.

"Oh, yes, we can." Ari kissed him. "Have you noticed that every time we're together, we spend the whole time making out? I wonder if that's healthy."

Cos laughed. "It's pretty normal. What do you think we ought to be doing? Talking about the national debt?"

"We do talk, though. Sometimes." Ari looked thoughtful. "Paul's attraction to Susannah is purely physical. I don't think they're friends the way we are."

Paul froze. It was a scene from the past. Susannah was long dead. He had killed her—and he didn't like being reminded of it. The image on the plate grew indistinct and pale, and gradually he became aware that he was staring once more at the blank surface of the gold. Ari and her boyfriend had vanished. Funny. Just as he had recoiled, the image had disappeared. It was as if it were some projection of his own mind. His thumbnail scraped at the shiny surface of the plate, and he puzzled over the mystery of how it worked.

Suddenly he stiffened. Cos! Why hadn't he thought of that. If anybody in the world knew where Ari was, it would be he. And Paul knew where to find him. He had been at a party at Cos's house the night Verena had made him. He felt sick with the memory, and gradually he became aware that the plate was growing warm in his hands. To his horror his own face was mirrored back to him in the plate. He stared in disbelief, seeing his head fall to the side and a blurred mass of blond hair drift in front of it, as if some out-of-focus person had stepped directly in front of the lens of a camera. The blond head was moving. Suddenly he was sure it was Verena! She was biting into his flesh!

Paul threw the heavy plate at the chest. He heard it clang like a cymbal against the other gold. He fell to the floor. He lay panting on his back, averting his gaze from the open chest. He didn't want to see Verena or think about what she had done to him. He wanted Ari. And now he had an idea about how he could find her.

When Cos drove up to his house, he was surprised to see a black Jaguar parked at the curb beside the large tree that shaded his front yard. He had never seen it, so he didn't quite know what to make of it. He didn't think any of his parents' friends owned a Jaguar. But he wasn't thinking too clearly after working six hours straight at the library—the deadening effect of hard work was what he used to kill his pain. He sure wasn't up to empty socializing. The last thing he wanted was to make polite chitchat with his parents' company.

He walked wearily toward the front door.

"Hi!"

The voice made him jump. Cos spun around at once, but he didn't see anyone. Was he starting to imagine things?

A boy stepped out from behind the tree. The streetlamp gleamed on his black curls. His back was to the light, and his dark eyes glowed strangely. It was Ari's brother, Paul! Cos's flesh crawled. Suddenly he understood why the kids at school had been so suspicious of Paul.

"Jeez, you scared me," he said.

"I guess you've been out visiting Ari," Paul said in a strange voice. He turned a little, and Cos saw that hollow eyes and cheeks made his face a macabre parody of Ari's beauty. "Where are you hiding her, huh?" He smiled a little.

"You got the wrong guy," Cos said. "She's moved in with Rab. I figured you knew that."

"After the fire there was so much confusion—" Paul broke off. "We seem to have temporarily lost track of each other," he went on stiffly. "Do you have her address?"

"Rab's in the Charlottesville phone book," Cos said quickly. Then he turned and ran into the house. "Brookridge Apartments. Apartment two-oh-six-B."

He breathlessly slammed the door behind him. Feeling vaguely ashamed, he locked the deadbolt. Then he peered out the door's peephole. Paul's black Jaguar had disappeared.

Cos leaned against the door and sighed deeply. For the first time, he began to wonder if Paul had actually killed Susannah and Nadia the way the kids at school thought he had. He looked so strange! His white skin made him look as if he hadn't been out-of-doors in years. Could it be that he had some horrible disease? Leprosy or something?

No—that didn't make sense. Ari would have

stayed in close touch with her twin if he were sick. Cos's mind was spinning. Why had Paul needed Ari's number? Was it possible that they had gotten separated after the fire—the way he had said? Cos figured they would have looked desperately for each other, then clung together afterward.

Something weird was going on. Maybe Ari hadn't told her twin where she was living because she was trying to get away from him. Suddenly he wished he hadn't told Paul where she was.

"Cos," his mother called from upstairs. "Is that you?"

"Yeah. I'm coming," he yelled. He ran up the stairs.

He found his mother making a sandwich in the kitchen. "This year I'm determined to get an early start on the income tax," she said. "And I'm not going to do it all by myself the way I did last year, either."

"Mom, did you see that Jaguar parked out front?"

"The black sports car? Is that what you mean?"

"Yeah. Do you have any idea how long it's been there?"

"I'm not sure. I think it was there when I got back from the grocery store. Maybe it's Tom Harris's." His mother slathered mustard on a slice of pumpernickel and added a slice of ham. "I hear he's having a mid-life crisis."

She put the pieces of bread together.

Cos realized that Paul must have been parked outside his house for hours, waiting. What was going on?

"Did you get a lot done at the library?" his mother asked.

"Yeah, sure." Cos carried his books into his room, threw them onto his bed, and stared vacantly at the wall. Suddenly nothing made sense to him. He thought he had it all figured out, but now the pieces of the puzzle were starting to rearrange themselves in his mind. He kept thinking about the living room of Rab's apartment, re-creating it in his mind as if he were playing a game called What's Wrong with This Picture?

He remembered that in the living room area there had been one of those funny Oriental couches that folded into a bed. He could picture it, a white, soft-looking thing. A book had been facedown on it, and next to that was a pile of folded sheets and a bed pillow. He wondered why he hadn't seen the significance of that pile of bed linens before. Obviously somebody—Ari or Rab, one—was sleeping in the bedroom, and the other was sleeping on that couch. It seemed clear now: Ari didn't have anything going with Rab at all. She had simply gone to him for help.

Cos bit his lip, feeling like a fool. He couldn't even remember half of what he had shouted at Ari, but he had been left with the uncomfortable feeling that he had said some pretty extreme things. He had actually made her cry! Not that he hadn't had a right to be mad. He had! But what good had it done him? It wasn't as if he were happier after telling her off. He had never been so unhappy.

Wasn't it possible that Ari had had a good reason for behaving the way she had? Maybe if she were afraid not only of the kids at school, but also of Paul . . . It made a kind of sense for her to go into deep hiding and pretend to be dead. It was something he could understand, anyway. He fervently wished he hadn't told Paul where she was.

Cos groped in his desk drawer for the scrap of paper where he had jotted down Rab's address and phone number. When he found it, he dialed the number. It rang once, then a recorded message came on telling him the number had been disconnected. Impatiently Cos punched the redial button, but he got the same message. He put the phone down. Rab Barron hadn't struck him as the sort who would forget to pay his phone bill.

Cos dialed long-distance information and asked for Rab's number. "I'm sorry," said the operator. "That number is unpublished."

Cos was suddenly seized with fear. Had he put Ari in danger?

Paul drove his car into the lighted parking lot of the Brookridge Apartments in Charlottesville.

The rows of cars told him that hundreds of people must live in this vast complex. It was lucky Cos had given him Rab's apartment number. His heart thudded hard with anticipation as he ran up the stairs. *Closer. Nearer. The light of his heart—Ari!*

But when he bounded up to the apartment, he was startled to see that it was empty. Neither curtains nor blinds hung on the windows; the light from the hallway revealed a broom by the refrigerator and a couple of cardboard boxes. That was all. She was gone!

CHAPTER
THIRTEEN

COS WAITED FOR SYBIL IN THE HALL OUTSIDE HER chemistry class until the final bell rang.

"Cos!" She paled when she spotted him.

"Come on, Sybil." He took her arm. "It can't be as bad as that. I mean, I know I haven't been a bundle of laughs lately—but it hasn't gotten to the point that people actually pass out when they see me." He smiled as kids hurried past them.

"I . . . I was only surprised," she said. "Did you want particularly to talk to me?"

Cos guided her firmly out the door. "Do yourself a favor and don't sign up for the CIA. You'd make a terrible spy. All I have to do is look at you to know you're hiding something."

"No!" she protested weakly. "I'm not hiding anything!"

He grinned. "Then you have no objection at

135

all if I buy you some hot chocolate, right?"

"Okay," she said, hunching her shoulders against the cold. The sky was overcast, and dry leaves spun down the walkway as they left the campus.

Cos took her to a snack shop on Massachusetts Avenue. He was careful to choose a table a good distance from the door. Not that he really thought Sybil would jump up and run out on him—but it didn't do any harm to make it hard for her.

"So, how was the chemistry test?" asked Cos.

Sybil stared at him. "Fine," she said.

"Okay, Syb—let's quit playing around." He laughed bitterly. "You know I don't care about your chemistry test. I only wanted to ask you if you knew where Ari is these days."

"I don't know." She shook her head. "After I told you that she was still alive, Rab was so mad he won't even give me his new address."

Cos found himself getting annoyed. Who did Rab think he was? "If you don't know anything, then why do you look so guilty?" he asked. He scrutinized every movement of Sybil's face. "Now, what could you be hiding?" Cos mused aloud. "Have you talked to Ari? Has she phoned?"

"She hasn't phoned," Sybil said, looking relieved.

Cos noticed her careful wording. He was pretty sure the words were true, but there had been a lot left unsaid. "Maybe *you* were the one who phoned *her*. . . . No!" he said, watching Sybil's face. "You haven't talked to her on the phone—you've *seen* her!" He knew at once by her confusion that he had gotten it right. For all he knew, Ari could be back in town! After all, she couldn't expect to camp at Rab's place forever. He reached over the table and grabbed Sybil's wrist. "When did you see her, Syb? What did she say?"

"Are you ready to order?" asked the waitress.

Cos glanced at the waitress ruefully and released Sybil. She turned away from him with obvious relief and ordered hot chocolate and a plate of cookies.

"And for you, sir?" asked the waitress.

"The same," he said shortly.

As soon as the waitress left, he returned his attention to Sybil. "Okay, where is she?"

"I don't know what you're talking about." Sybil's eyes avoided his.

In spite of himself Cos was beginning to see the funny side of this KGB-style interrogation. From the way Sybil was acting, anybody would think he had a knife at her throat. He grinned suddenly. "What's the big deal, Syb? I know you saw her. You know that I know you saw her. How can it hurt for you to tell me the truth?"

"I ran into her by accident," Sybil admitted suddenly. "It turned out she had to come into town to make out a statement for the police about the fire. I found out about it because I picked up the phone at home and heard my dad setting up the appointment. So I went to the police station and waited there until she came out." Sybil smiled a little. "It was fun—we went downtown together and had ice cream."

The waitress put cups of steaming chocolate before them, but Cos scarcely looked at his. He felt depressed. How come Sybil had gotten to see Ari and he hadn't? Suddenly the touch and smell of Ari came back to him so sharply he had to catch his breath.

"I don't know where she went after that," Sybil added.

He'd had his chance to see Ari, he reminded himself—but he had blown it. Why would she want to talk to him again after the way he had lost his temper?

"Don't turn around," Sybil suddenly whispered. "Jessie just came in with Amanda."

Cos winced. Right. Jessie and Amanda. His life used to be simple—he'd had a girl, lots of friends, decent grades, and he never seemed to worry at all. Now Ari had vanished, and he wasn't on speaking terms with half the school—including Jessie and Amanda. He was careful not to turn around and look at them.

"I guess Ari didn't mention me, did she?" he asked.

"Yes, she did," Sybil admitted. "She asked how you were. I told her you had lost your sense of humor."

"Maybe you're right about that." He stirred his chocolate, aware of the somber lines of disappointment that had appeared on his face. "Well, if you hear from her again," he said, "tell her I'm sorry I said all those things, and I'd really like to see her."

Sybil eyed him uneasily. "Why are you so anxious to know where Ari is all of a sudden?"

Cos glanced over his shoulder and caught Jessie looking at him. When Jessie realized Cos had spotted him, he looked down at once and pretended to be studying the menu.

He lowered his voice. "Last night, Paul came to my house looking for Ari."

Sybil looked surprised. "He must have lost track of her somehow. He went to live with their dad, you see. Ari doesn't get along with their dad."

"It hasn't hit you that maybe she's hiding from Paul?"

"Oh, no, Cos!" Sybil exclaimed. "You've got it wrong. Paul and Ari have always been very close."

Cos cast another cautious glance over his shoulder. "But what if Ari knows that Paul is a murderer?" he whispered.

"No!" hissed Sybil. "He's not! Whoever murdered Susannah and Nadia was a homicidal maniac. Paul isn't like that at all!"

"He gives me the creeps, Syb. I can't even describe the way he looks."

"You know what the trouble is?" said Sybil. "You've let those rumors get to you. Next thing you'll be telling me Paul and Ari are vampires. All

139

that talk is wicked. Look how it ended up—with a mob going to Ari's house and killing her aunt. It's so horrible!" She shuddered and cast an uneasy glance over Cos's shoulder at Amanda and Jessie. "How can they sit over there acting like they haven't done anything wrong? It just amazes me. Everybody knows Jessie was behind it."

But Cos was beginning to wonder if Jessie's suspicions of Paul were more soundly based than he had thought. He couldn't forget the chill he had felt when Paul had shown up last night. "I wish Ari were here in town," he said miserably. "I'd just like to see for myself that she's okay."

"She'll be okay as long as she's with Rab," said Sybil. "He'll take good care of her."

A slight drizzle had begun outside the snack shop. Cos felt sick as he thought of how he had given Rab's address to Paul last night. "Let's hope you're right," he muttered.

Paul awoke with a start. He lay on top of Sophie, his chest rising and falling with her breathing. Tentatively he crooked his elbow and lifted the coffin lid a little. It was dark in the room, and he could hear rain pelting against the windows. He pushed the top open and rolled off of Sophie.

She sat up, rubbing her eyes. "Is it raining?" Her skin was taut over her cheekbones, and her lips were a ghastly white. "It sounds like a storm."

Thunder rumbled. Paul parted the blinds and peeked out. "Yeah, I think it is a storm. It's awfully dark out there, and the rain's really coming down. I expect it's settled in for the rest of the afternoon."

Paul's mouth fell open as he gazed in fascination at the street below. Everything was gray and the outlines of the cars below were blurred in the downpour.

"Let's go for a walk," Sophie whispered.

The thunder had stirred a sense of urgency in Paul, too, but something held him at the window. He watched two figures on the sidewalk below struggling against the wind. The boy opened a car door, then glanced up at the apartment window. Paul drew back. "Jeez," he said. "That's my sister's boyfriend. I should have known—that looks like his car."

Sophie hastily smoothed lipstick on her pale lips. "Okay," she said. "I'm ready."

"I better stay here," said Paul. "You go on without me."

"You aren't worried about them, are you? They'll be driving off in a minute."

"Yeah, but we're right across the street from my old school." Paul glanced at his watch. "School must have just let out. No telling who I might run into out there." But seeing Sophie's eyes darken with disappointment, he suddenly decided not to worry. "You're right—let's go." They went downstairs and stepped out into the rain, and at once his jeans were soaked. The umbrella wasn't much use; rain drummed deafeningly loudly on it, and a thin spray peppered his face through its fabric. Paul was glad to see no sign of Cos's car. An image flashed through his mind of a mob forming at St. Anselm's and crossing the street to torch Sophie's apartment. He could never let that happen—Sophie was too precious to him. Her face, under her red umbrella, looked surprisingly pink, and Paul touched her cheek tenderly.

Suddenly a fork of lightning flashed to the north, and a crack of thunder sounded. Sophie shot him a frightened look. "I wonder what would happen if lightning hit us."

"It'd be curtains for us," said Paul. "Maybe it would be for the best."

"Don't say that," she whispered.

Paul looked around him. Sheets of water surged along the edges of the street. He couldn't shake the black depression that hung over him. It was his grief over losing Ari, he supposed. He had to stop thinking about her.

Paul folded up his umbrella just as a slender blond boy stepped out of the school's Activities Building. He looked directly at them both and stiffened.

Paul swore. "I can't believe it," he said, grabbing Sophie's arm.

"What's wrong?" asked Sophie.

Paul pulled her into a nearby alley. "That was Jessie Driscoll." He was annoyed to realize he was rattled.

142

"Is he somebody you used to go to school with?"

"Yeah, he hates me," said Paul briefly. "He's already tried to kill me twice."

Sophie's eyes widened in alarm. "Do you think he saw you?"

"I'm not sure." Paul craned his neck to peer at the Activities Building. Rain plastered the hair to his head. There was no sign of Jessie now. "You better go back to the apartment." He raised his voice above the storm. "I want to make sure I've lost him before I go inside. I don't want to risk leading him to our apartment."

"I'm afraid," whimpered Sophie. "I don't want to leave you, Paul. Take me with you."

He grinned suddenly. "Don't worry." He gave her a little shove. "I'll be back before you know it."

She glanced back at him as she stepped out of the alley. Paul raised his hand in a rueful salute. When she had gone, he turned and ran toward the school.

Paul already regretted ditching his umbrella. Rain streamed into his eyes as he stepped out on the street. Water rushed over his sneakers. The downpour was furious. He gingerly felt his way between parked cars. He could make out a blur of approaching headlights, but they were going slow. When he stepped from between the parked cars, however, he heard a sudden roar and looked up to see that the car was coming at him full speed.

Before he realized what had happened, he felt the blow and found himself scooped up on its hood. His face pressed against the windshield. He could see Jessie behind the wheel, his expression one of sheer terror.

Suddenly the car careened out of control, and Paul was flung onto the street. He heard the car crash, an explosion of metal and glass. When he turned, he saw Jessie's car had hit a brick building. Its hood was folded up like an accordion, and its battery hung out, dangling loosely over the crumpled metal. The windows were opaque webs of cracked glass.

Paul leapt to his feet. He could feel rain on his bare, scraped knees as he made his way over to the car—but the rain didn't bother him now. The thought of Jessie trapped inside the car made his pulse pound in his ears louder than the rain.

He had waited a long time to get his hands on Jessie Driscoll.

The car door was jammed. Paul drove his fist through the window. When his hand touched Jessie's warm body, he felt a shiver of pleasure, and his body trembled in anticipation.

He butted his head at the shattered glass and found himself hanging in the car, nose-to-nose with Jessie. Jessie's eyes were closed. He was still breathing, but his face was badly cut up, and blood streamed into his eyes. For an instant Paul froze, transfixed by the blood. Then he grabbed Jessie under his arms and pulled.

Nothing happened. He needed more leverage. Rocking back out of the window, he braced himself and tried the jammed door again. This time it flew open. He dragged Jessie out of the car and knelt beside him. He smiled. His enemy was still alive; that meant he could have the pleasure of drinking his warm blood.

Paul braced himself with his toes against the wet pavement and struck Jessie's neck with bruising force.

He saw the rain splashing on the street around him as he felt Jessie's legs twitch spasmodically. Then he closed his eyes, shutting out the sights and sound of the downpour. He wanted only to feel his body rocking to the beat of Jessie's heart. Waves of warmth lapped him, and as Paul gulped down the blood, he felt more than brute pleasure; he felt a flutter of jubilation. With every weakening heartbeat, Jessie's life was ebbing away from him.

The distant sound of a siren made Paul raise his head. Uneasiness stirred in him, and he realized that he felt heat behind him—heat where there should only have been cold rain. Glancing over his shoulder, he spotted the ominous flicker of flame inside the wrecked car.

Suddenly a man shouted in Paul's ear: "We've got to get him away from the car. It may blow up." The man grabbed Jessie's arms and dragged him away. With detachment, Paul noticed that the rushing rain had washed Jessie's face clean of blood. Still, his enemy looked strangely unlike himself, with his blond hair swept back and his jaw hanging slack. If any ember of life still burned in him, it had to be very weak.

Paul stood up. He felt as if he were moving in slow motion. Somehow he managed to stumble away from the burning car. He felt the force of the rain and knew that it must have been helping hide him from view as he slid into the dark alley. There he leaned his forehead against the wall to catch his breath. His cheeks felt hot. "Jeez," he muttered, catching himself against the wall. The siren was close now. He tensed, waiting for the explosion. Instead, the siren whined and wound down. He heard excited voices, but no explosion.

He felt a mild resentment toward the Good Samaritan for interrupting him at the kill, but he knew it was just as well he had gotten away when he did. The last thing he needed was a brush with the law.

He stepped out of the alley on the other side and looked up and down the street that ran in front of his building. The trees and lawns of St. Anselm's were pastel in the slanting rain. A single station wagon pulled out of the circular drive, but the campus was almost deserted.

Paul streamed a trail of water as he went into his apartment building. He walked upstairs slowly, but a smile played on his lips as he thought of the scene on the street below. Jessie had been in bad shape after the crash—he was unlikely to survive. Though Paul had been in a frenzy at the time, he was conscious that he must have drunk a lot of blood. His arms and even his lips felt thick and warm with the pleasure of heavy feeding. Jessie was dead. He had to be.

Sophie flung the apartment door open and regarded him with wide eyes. "Paul, are you all right? I heard something that sounded like a bomb."

Paul didn't bother to explain. "I'm great," he smiled. "Absolutely great!" He enfolded her in his arms and drew her close. As he nuzzled her, his tongue flicked out and skated lightly along the long blue vein in her neck.

Sophie shivered. "Good grief, Paul. Your breath stinks of blood. What have you been up to? You didn't attack a cop, did you?"

Paul realized she must have heard the sirens. "No, even better than that!" He grinned. "Jeez, I feel on top of the world." He gripped her shoulder. "Wait here a minute." He went into the bedroom, closing the door behind him, and unlatched the chest. Groping in it a moment, he found the small black bag he was looking for. He tipped it so that some delicate pieces of gold fell into his palm. Paul plucked out a gold ring with an azure stone, then slid the rest of the ornaments back in the bag. The ring's gold was dull—not like highly polished modern gold—giving it a soft look.

Paul went back to the living room and laid it in her hand.

"Oh, Paul," she cried. "It's beautiful."

He looked into her blue eyes. He squeezed her hands tightly in his. "With this ring, I pledge my love," he said huskily.

Sophie sniffled and then burst into tears.

Paul blinked and took a step back. "Does that scare you or something?"

"No!" she cried. "It's just that I'm so happy."

"Oh." He smiled, noticing she had bent her finger to keep the ring from falling off. "I guess you'll want to have it taken in," he said. He'd almost said, "find a discreet jeweler," but had stopped himself in time. He didn't want Sophie to think the ring was hot. That would spoil the romance of the moment.

"I can't wait to show everybody!" said Sophie, waving her hand jubilantly over her head.

Paul closed his eyes. He hoped she didn't show Verena. But he couldn't worry about that now. He had taken care of Jessie. That was enough for one day.

CHAPTER
FOURTEEN

COS GRABBED THE PHONE BEFORE IT HAD A CHANCE
to ring a second time.

"Cos?" Sybil's voice came over the wire.
"Something terrible's happened."

His heart stopped. "It's not Ari, is it?"

"No, it's Jessie," she cried. "Turn on the TV.
Channel Fourteen."

The receiver clicked and Sybil was gone. Cos
held the humming phone in his hand.

He switched on the TV. It showed the
charred skeleton of a car that had crashed into a
building.

"—the scene this afternoon," a voice in-
toned, "when a high-speed crash took the life
of a St. Anselm's student and son of TIC execu-
tive Michael Driscoll. Jessie Driscoll, seventeen, was alone when he lost control of his '94
Chevrolet Camaro and crashed into Parkside

Apartments. Witnesses report that an unidentified bystander broke the windows of the wrecked vehicle and pulled Driscoll from the wreckage seconds before the car burst into flames. The unknown rescuer also attempted CPR, say witnesses, but Driscoll was pronounced dead at the scene. Driscoll had been hospitalized briefly after the death of his girlfriend, murder victim Nadia Tanasescu, but a family spokesman reports that he had made a good recovery from his depression and had been in excellent spirits for the past few weeks. The police are investigating whether a mechanical failure could be at fault."

Cos stared at the screen for some time. When he realized he was staring blindly at a weather map, he switched it off.

Cos heard the front door open and bounded down the stairs. "Dad! Jessie's dead!"

His father paused in the hallway. His face was dark. "I know. Somebody at the office heard it on the radio. I just came from the Driscolls'. I think you'd better call on them tomorrow. It would mean a lot to them."

His father went into the kitchen and poured himself a tall glass of orange juice. He leaned his forehead against the refrigerator. "I remember riding Jessie around on my shoulders when he wasn't any more than two," he said softly. "He was the most beautiful child I ever saw. It just doesn't seem possible."

His father was right—it didn't seem possible.

Cos perched on a kitchen stool, frowning. First Susannah, then Nadia. Now Jessie. But Jessie's wreck had been an accident, not murder. "Dad," he said, "there wasn't anything suspicious about Jessie's wreck, was there?"

"Maybe the accelerator jammed?" suggested his father. He shook his head. "I guess we may never know."

"I'm going over to Sybil's," Cos announced. "I won't be out late."

"I wish you wouldn't, Cos. The roads are still slick."

"I'll be careful." He had started down the stairs. He didn't push his luck by making a slow exit. He was afraid his mother would come in and make him stay home.

As he drove to Sybil's, he found himself checking the rearview mirror constantly. His senses were numb except for a vague nervousness. He wasn't even sure why he was worried, but he felt uneasy in his skin. Jumpy.

When he got to the Barrons' house, Sybil came to the door. At the sight of him she burst into tears. She leaned on him, heaving with ugly sobs. Cos found his own eyes prickling with tears. It was strange, because he had barely spoken to Jess since the fire. They had once been good friends—and he hadn't even had a chance to talk things out or patch things up. It was hard for him to imagine a world without Jessie.

"I feel sick," sniffled Sybil. She staggered into

the living room, swabbing at her eyes vigorously with a sodden tissue.

Cos sat down on the couch and stared at the nearby arrangement of family pictures in silver frames. Cos found himself staring particularly at one with Rab. He was half a head taller than his father and had a frizzy mane of hair like Sybil's, but his hair was sooty black. He was the darkest of the Barrons. Even in his miserable frame of mind, Cos was troubled by the sense that something didn't fit.

"What do you think this means, Syb?" he blurted suddenly.

She blew her nose. "Jessie's wreck? What can it possibly mean? Nothing. Sometimes awful things happen, that's all."

"Don't you think the car crash seems a little neat?"

"Neat?" Sybil looked confused. "You saw the car, Cos. It was a mess. And poor Jessie—"

"Not the wreck," said Cos impatiently. "I mean, the fact that Jessie died. He set out to get even for Nadia's and Susannah's murders, and suddenly he's dead. It's like a perfect circle—don't you see? Too neat."

Sybil stared. "Are you saying somebody is pulling strings to make all these things happen?"

"Didn't you recognize where the crash was? It was on Fulton Street—only a block from the school. Jessie must have just left school when it happened."

Sybil dabbed at her eyes. "What's your point?"

"My point is, what was he doing speeding there? The entire street is only about two and a half blocks long. It would be pretty hard to get up speed in that distance."

"Camaros have a lot of pickup," gulped Sybil.

"Are you saying Jessie just revved up his car and drove into a brick wall?"

Sybil jumped. "Suicide? Oh, I don't think so. Do you? He'd been on top of the world lately."

Yeah, thought Cos bitterly. *Since he burned Ari's house down.* "I wonder if there were any skid marks," he said. "The trouble is, with all that rain, any evidence there was is probably gone."

"What kind of evidence are you talking about? It was just a car crash. Listen, Cos—your imagination is running away with you."

"I sure would like to know more about that guy that pulled Jess out of the car."

"I think what he did was wonderful," Sybil said. "That way Jessie's parents don't have to wonder, you know, if he could have been saved. Somebody was right there and did everything that could possibly have been done."

"Maybe," muttered Cos.

"What are you getting at?" cried Sybil.

"I don't know." Cos looked at her helplessly. "I just don't know."

Paul found himself looking forward to

153

Sophie's going to work every night. Then he would take the gold out of the chest and run his fingers lovingly over every piece. Tonight Paul sat cross-legged on the bedroom floor and lined the gold up in a circle around him—plates, chalices, thin disks, delicate masks. *All this gold and I've barely tapped its powers!*

Picking up a jeweled plate, Paul rubbed it, letting his thumb make squeaking noises on the slick surface. The plate grew warm under his thumb, and suddenly an image leapt to life on it. But the colors were dark and strange. Paul shook it impatiently, hoping to bring it into sharper focus. He could barely make out what was going on. He held it close to his face. It looked as if a man were lying in a rough bed of tall weeds. Paul could see a single boot poking through the maroon stems. Suddenly Paul realized that the figure's head was jerking. Paul recognized the frantic motion of a vampire tearing flesh, and his mouth watered. The thrashing that stirred the weeds set his imagination aflame, and he stared hungrily at the action.

Suddenly Paul's father's face was framed in the jeweled circle, as real as if Richard were looking through a porthole. *He's dead,* Paul reminded himself, trying to quiet his pounding heart. Richard's high-arched black brows looked spiky, damp with blood, and his glistening lips pursed into a tight circle as if he were saying, "Oh!" He pulled his lips back, baring his fangs,

154

and suddenly the angle changed. Paul saw the delicate jawline of the victim and a brutal tear in the neck just below the jawbone. The flesh gaped and blood spurted out of it in the rhythm of a heartbeat.

A flutter of desire moved in Paul's stomach at the thought of the warm fountain of blood. The image panned away from the wound then, and Paul saw in tight close-up a view of smooth and rounded cheeks. Not Richard's, surely. Someone very much younger. Paul caught a glimpse of dark hair over a delicate ear. It was Sophie's face!

Paul rose to his knees in sudden shock. "I'm not going to watch anymore," he said aloud, but his fingers had a tight grip on the plate, and his gaze was drawn to it as if strong hands held his skull in a viselike grip. He couldn't look away, even though anguished sweat was beading on his brow. He watched Richard's long teeth plunge into Sophie's neck, his lips pressing tightly against the torn flesh.

Paul's heart twisted as he stared at Sophie. Her face's contours were soft and warmer than he remembered. And she had gentle, frightened eyes. She was so young! Sweat had beaded above her lip. A thick, white bar, out of focus, suddenly swung over her mouth, blocking Paul's view, and with a start Paul realized it must be Richard's arm. Richard had slashed his own flesh and was going to offer his blood. Sophie's eyes were unfocused, but suddenly, to Paul's horror, he could see the strained muscles at the front of her neck as she lifted her head up to press her mouth desperately against Richard's wrist.

Horrified, Paul watched as the bones on her cheeks grew sharp, pressing against the skin. Her flesh seemed to shrink, growing hard and tight against the delicate bones of her skull. And then her eyes began to change. Paul felt tears on his cheeks as her eyes hardened and turned to gems. A cold starlike sparkle appeared in their depths. Vampire eyes.

Paul flung the plate away from him violently. It struck the wall and fell, clanging like a cymbal to the floor. He squeezed his eyes closed. *It's sick to keep thinking about it. It's in the past. It doesn't have anything to do with me. So Sophie is a vampire—so what? So am I. And there's only one way to become one, isn't there? I knew that already. So what's my problem?*

But the voice of reason in Paul's head grew fainter as he clutched his hands to his throbbing temples, and suddenly he fell to his hands and knees and crawled to the fallen plate. He picked it up, panting, afraid it was broken. A jewel tumbled to the floor. Paul picked it up between his thumb and forefinger and tried to press it back into its place. The shiny surface of the plate was dented, and he stroked it tenderly. He felt his heart give a queer leap as it warmed. The gold darkened, its shine obscured by dark colors—purple, red, green. An image was coalescing, shapeless at first, but slowly coming into focus. Two vampires were embracing, and the dark surface behind them was painted with poisonous-looking flowers and fluorescent insects. Paul recognized the wall of an offbeat club where Sophie had taken him a couple of times. It was Sophie and Dubay! He watched as Sophie threw back her head, exposing her long throat. Dubay plucked at it gently with his fangs, pinching the hard skin. Abruptly he bit hard, and Paul saw Sophie's body quiver.

Paul pressed the plate facedown on the floor and threw himself down over it, sobbing. The loose jewel rolled against a baseboard and winked at him coldly in the light. He burst into tears.

"I can't stand it!"

CHAPTER
FIFTEEN

WHEN SOPHIE GOT HOME, PAUL WAS SITTING ON THE couch, reading. "Hi," he said, glancing up. "Did you show everybody the ring I gave you?"

"Yes." She gave him an uneasy glance. "You didn't say that I shouldn't."

"Oh, go ahead." He waved a hand carelessly. "I guess you want all your friends to know you've got me roped and tied. How many hearts have you collected now, Sophie? Ten? Twenty?"

Sophie seemed stunned by his anger. "Is something wrong, Paul? Have I done something to make you mad at me?"

"Let's talk," said Paul sarcastically. "Communication is the key, right? That's what you're always telling me."

Her eyes were fixed on him anxiously.

"I think we ought to talk about when my father made you into a vampire." His voice was poisonously soft. "What was it like for you? Tell me everything."

Sophie licked her lips.

"What's the matter—don't you remember?"

"I don't want to talk about it. It was awful."

"Not so awful that you spit out his stinking blood!" Paul shouted. He could feel his temples pounding, and he knew he shouldn't say any more, but everything he said made sense! Sophie couldn't argue with facts. She had drunk his father's blood. Nobody had made her. Worse, she had been *hungry* for it. He had seen the look on her face as she had fed on Richard.

"Richard murdered me," Sophie said. "And now you're saying that what he did to me was my fault. Well, go ahead and say whatever you want—I can't stop you. But don't expect me to agree with you. I was the victim!"

"Some victim," snorted Paul. "What about Dubay?"

"What about Dubay? Whatever I did with Dubay doesn't have anything to do with you."

"Oh, yes, it does!" Paul yelled. "And you know why?" He jabbed a finger at her. "Because it means I can't trust you, Sophie."

"I won't let you talk to me that way," said Sophie, tears welling up in her eyes

"Oh, you won't?" Paul slapped her.

Her head snapped back, and he watched his phosphorescent handprint form on her cheek. Suddenly he punched her hard in the stomach, and she doubled over. She fell down, weeping brokenly.

He knelt beside her, tears running down his cheeks. "Why do you make me do this?" he cried. "I love you, but you make me crazy."

"Get away from me!" she choked, pushing him. "If you touch me again, I'll tell Dubay."

Paul recoiled. In his heart he didn't believe that Sophie still cared for Dubay; her words shocked him.

She struggled to her feet and staggered into the bathroom. Feeling sick to his stomach, he listened to the water running.

He stood at the door and waited until she came out. "I'm sorry," he whispered.

She didn't answer him.

"I didn't mean it," he pleaded. "I don't know what makes me act that way."

Sophie stuffed a wallet and comb into a little purse. Her lips were tight.

"Where are you going?" he asked.

"None of your business."

"Are . . . are you going to Dubay's?"

"Paul!" she screamed. "Stop it!"

"Well, you did mention him," he said. "Are you two still seeing each other?"

"No, we're not. But I guess you don't believe that. You have a serious problem—you know that?"

"I know. Don't go, Sophie. I can't stand it if you do. I love you so much, it just makes me insane sometimes."

"I'm not making you act this way, Paul. You're the one who's doing it to yourself." Sophie snapped the purse shut.

"No, it's Ari." Paul buried his face in his hands. "I miss her so much! Everything is going to be different once I get back with Ari. She always kept me straight. Now that she's not around, I'm spinning around not knowing what I'm doing. I'm losing my balance, because I miss her so much. Once I find her, everything will be all right."

Sophie frowned. "But you don't have any idea where she is."

"Oh, I'll find her," said Paul quickly. "I've got a plan. And once I catch up with her, I'll make her into a vampire. Then all three of us can live together. That would be okay with you, wouldn't it?"

"I don't know, Paul." Sophie fingered her cheek. "All I can think about right now is whether things are going to work out between you and me."

"It'll be different. You'll see. Once Ari is here, it'll be completely different. I'll have what I want then." He bit his lip. "Then I won't act so nuts."

She opened the door.

"When will you be back?" he asked.

She shrugged.

"By dawn?"

"I don't know!" she cried. "Leave me alone."

"I'll come with you!"

"No!"

"Well, what do you expect me to do while you're out running around?"

"That's your problem." Sophie blew her nose. "I think you must not love me at all or you wouldn't treat me this way—that's what I think!"

"No, Sophie," he protested, reaching for her. "I do love you!"

"Don't touch me!" She pulled away and slammed the door in his face.

Ari took one last look at herself in the rear-view mirror before she got out. The black T-shirt seemed to drain the flesh color from her face, and a dusting of baby powder made her skin even more pale. Through the fluorescent lenses she looked vaguely shiny and lavender-tinted. A muscle under her eye twitched, a tell-tale sign of nervous strain.

She took a deep breath as she got out of the car. She couldn't deny her fright. But she stood up, straightened her shoulders, and walked boldly toward the open door of the vampire bar.

She was jolted when she saw two skinny women step out arm in arm. Aunt Gabrielle's friends Gwen and Tippi! Gwen's pipestem legs were tightly encased in sand-colored pants, and over them she wore a translucent tunic. Tippi was in a loosely woven dress that reminded Ari of the color of mushrooms. Around her neck and wrists was heavy beaded and knotted jewelry.

"Ari!" Gwen squealed. "How utterly lovely to see you. I thought you had left town. What are you doing around here?"

"Looking for Paul," Ari admitted.

"He should be easy to find. We talked to him the other night. Didn't we, Tippi?"

Tippi touched a tissue to her eyes. "We expressed our sympathy about poor Gabrielle."

"Poor, dear child," said Gwen, putting a bony hand on Ari's shoulder. "Such a loss. Of course, we'll tell Paul you're looking for him."

Ari gulped. "Maybe you'd better not mention it. I . . . I want to surprise him."

Gwen looked at her sharply. "You realize he's living with his girlfriend, don't you?"

Ari shook her head.

"What's her name?" Gwen snapped bony fingers. "Sophie. That's it. Maybe it is better to feel your way. Threesomes so seldom work out."

Tippi giggled. "Have you decided to come over and become one of us? Gwenny and I would be happy to oblige if you're interested. We could do a sort of duet."

Ari felt herself go cold as Gwenny squeezed her shoulder. "Now, now, dear, don't be frightened. You aren't frightened of us, are you?"

"She's petrified," said Tippi. "Look at her face—white as a sheet."

"No, that's only powder. So cute! She's going to try to pass! Look at the adorable contact lenses, Tippi! Don't you love them!" Gwenny laughed. "Well, we'll keep your little secret.

Never fear. So you're going in there?" She jerked her head toward the open door.

"I guess so." Ari darted a nervous glance toward the open bar. She wished Gwen would shut up. What if someone inside should overhear what they were saying?

"You're taking a risk," said Tippi. "Not all those guys in there are liberals like Gwenny and me."

"Now leave her alone, Tippi," scolded Gwen. "The girl *loves* risks. She's Richard's daughter, remember. Good luck, dear. We wish you all the best whichever way you swing. Don't we, Tippi?" The two vampires walked away giggling, arm in arm.

Ari was so scared, she was afraid she might pass out, but she forced herself to step inside. At first she could see nothing. Her eyes had not adjusted to the darkness. She stood in the doorway, trembling and confused. She longed for a match, a lighter—anything with which to defend herself. Why hadn't she thought of that?

In the gloom she made out glimpses of white, pointed chins, strangely glowing eyes, and skinny bodies. A full-busted girl with a silken fringe of blond hair brushed by her. Verena! She could never forget those sinister green eyes. Ari turned quickly and slid onto the nearest bar stool. She was startled when she realized that her pale face in the mirror behind the bartender was indistinguishable from the other faces. It was painfully evident that her cheeks had grown hollow from worrying about Paul.

The bartender's long white face turned toward her as he took her measure. Then, without speaking, he slid a glass of red liquid toward her. She supposed she should be relieved that he seemed to accept her as a vampire, but she gazed down at her glass with repulsion. The liquid clung to the sides of the glass. It had begun to coagulate at its surface. Blood. Maybe she should drink it, but her stomach turned at the thought. She vaguely remembered that the Masai tribe drank cow's blood, and the Mongols had drunk horse blood. But these historical footnotes weren't much comfort. She licked her lips and looked up and down the bar desperately, wondering how she should pay the bartender. Surreptitiously, she glanced at the vampire beside her and noticed she had laid some bills on the bar. Ari quickly laid some bills beside her glass.

A strobe light swept the room, and Ari caught glimpses of nightmarish dead faces swimming in the darkness behind her. Bursts of raucous laughter sounded over the brutal thump of the music. Her breath had begun to come in gasps. She knew now that she could never make herself turn around and look directly at the crowded room behind her. What if they suddenly realized she was human? What if they attacked her?

She gripped the edge of the bar and tried to

166

make herself breathe evenly. If she just got out of here alive, she vowed, she would never try anything this stupid again.

The girl on the stool next to her was twirling a ring around her finger. Ari found she could not take her eyes off the ring for some reason. It was the same dull gold as the magic chalice.

"That's an interesting ring," Ari blurted out.

A tear left a shiny path on the girl's white cheek. "It doesn't fit. I'll have to have it made smaller. Maybe."

"C-could I take a look at it?"

The girl took it off and slid it over. Ari's fluorescent contact lenses made it hard for her to make out details in the dim light, and she had to hold the ring close to her eyes and turn it slowly in her fingers. No question—the design was the same as on the chalice; even the tiny embossed figures were the same: a stylized falcon holding its helpless prey.

Her heart pounded so hard she felt dizzy. "My name is Anne," she said impulsively, using a short version of her given name. She glanced at the face of the girl next to her. "What's yours?"

"Sophie." The girl smiled.

Ari jumped. This vampire was Paul's girlfriend. How strange to be talking to the one who could lead her to Paul!

"I don't like to pry." Ari uneasily fingered her glass. "But you look upset. Is something wrong?"

"It's my boyfriend," Sophie whispered. "He's

167

pathologically jealous. Have you ever known somebody like that?"

She shook her head.

"You're lucky," said Sophie, touching her hand to her cheek. "It's awful. When he gets jealous he slaps me around."

"He *hit* you?" Ari stared at her, appalled.

Sophie nodded. "Sometimes I ask myself if I ought to get out of this thing while I still can."

"Yes," said Ari. "You should." She had the eerie sensation that she was talking about someone else, not Paul. She had read about abusive relationships, but she had always figured the people involved in them must be deeply strange. Of course Paul and his girlfriend were deeply strange, she reminded herself. They were vampires. The girl before her had eyes like a cat, eyes that glowed an icy blue in the gloom. Her face was as white as death and the telltale gold ring hung on a bony finger. Her mouth was slightly open, and a fang pressed against her lower lip. Ari found herself gazing in fascination at Sophie's mouth.

"He really loves me," said Sophie. "I don't know." She toyed with the ring. "Vampire love has a lot of pain." Her cat eyes met Ari's. "You know?"

"Uh, yes," stuttered Ari. "Of course."

"You're so pretty. I'm sure you've had lots of boyfriends." Sophie sighed. "When he rips my neck it hurts, but then I hurt him back, and that's cool because just when it hurts most is when I feel almost alive." She looked down, embarrassed. "I hate to think I'm turning into one of those awful hags that buttonholes strangers at bars."

"Oh, no!" Ari gulped. "I'm very interested."

Sophie's eyes darkened until they looked like dull blue stones. "I just can't stand it when he calls me names and tells me he can't t-trust me and all." She laid her head down on her arms and her thin shoulders heaved.

"There, there." Normally Ari might have patted the girl on the shoulder, but she was afraid to touch her. "You'll work it out," she said weakly. *This is a nightmare! This vampire—this pathetic and frightening creature beside me—is Paul's girlfriend!* Ari scarcely knew what to make of the dark glimpse she had gotten of Sophie and Paul's life together. Was it actually possible that Paul had hit this frail creature?

Sophie straightened up, sniffling. "I love him so much. He says everything will be different when his sister comes to live with us. Then things will be back to normal."

"H-his sister is coming to live with you?" Ari choked. "But what if his sister doesn't want to become a vampire!"

Sophie blinked. "How did you guess that she's not a vampire?"

"You mentioned it," said Ari swiftly.

"Did I?" Sophie looked puzzled. "No, I'm sure I didn't. You must be telepathic."

"Sometimes," said Ari, relieved that Sophie had provided an excuse for her slip.

"That must be it, then." Sophie sighed. "You read my thoughts."

"But what if she doesn't want to be a vampire?" Ari repeated urgently.

"Oh, he'll make her," said Sophie. "She pleaded with him once not to, and he let that stop him, but he won't this time. He won't let anything stop him now, because he sees that he can't do without her."

"You should talk him out of it," she whispered. "It would be wrong to force her."

Sophie shook her head. "When he makes her into a vampire, they'll be very close, the way a brother and sister should be. Besides, I know it would make him really happy."

Ari's fingers felt stiff. She felt herself growing cold and for a horrible second, when she looked up at the mirror, she had the sensation she was turning into a vampire, that her life was leaking out without her being able to do anything about it.

"The reason I think it would be okay," said Sophie earnestly, "is because he really loves her. That makes it different."

"If they're close, he should want what's best for her," said Ari. "You should tell him that."

"Oh, you can't reason with him when he's made up his mind. Besides, I think it may make all the difference for us, and we deserve some happiness!"

170

"But what about his sister?" cried Ari. "She deserves happiness, too!"

"Paul needs her," said Sophie sharply. "I don't see why she's too good to be a vampire. What makes her better than us? It's our turn to be happy. We've already been through so much." Sophie's fangs glistened in the darkness; her lips were stained with blood. "It's been so long since I've been able to talk like this. There's just something about you that's very *simpatico*. It's something about the wavelength you're on—" Sophie stared into Ari's eyes, and for a chilling moment Ari was afraid she was going to comment on Ari's resemblance to her twin. Instead she smiled. "Do you, by any chance, like poetry?"

Ari nodded. She could no longer trust herself to speak.

"I knew it!" cried Sophie. "Listen, I wonder if you'd like to come back to my place and meet Paul!" She grabbed Ari's hand, and Ari froze when she saw the other girl's expression change. Her eyes blank, Sophie reached up to lay cool finger's on Ari's neck. Ari cringed.

"You're warm!" Sophie whispered. "You're not a vampire!"

Ari leapt up suddenly.

"Ari!"

She glanced over her shoulder as the strobe light spotlighted Paul's face at the back of the bar. He was so tall, she could see him clearly over the crowd. His face was twisted into an expression of concentration, and she sensed he was pushing, trying desperately to get to her.

"*You* are Ari?" cried Sophie, aghast. "*You?*"

Ari edged desperately past a blond vampire. She felt something wet splash her shirt, but she didn't stop. It was horrifying to know she was surrounded by vampires and to wonder if they could somehow sense the heat of her body. The strobe light was disorienting. Ari was terrified she would fall.

"Excuse me, beautiful!" A vampire stepped in her way. Curling black hair peeked from the V in his shirt. She dodged him and pushed blindly toward the door. When at last she made it outside to the sidewalk, she broke into a run. She was conscious of people turning to stare as she bolted down the street, gasping for breath. Finally she reached the car. The motor coughed and began to roar. She pulled out at once into traffic amid the blare of protesting horns.

In the rearview mirror she caught a glimpse of Paul on the sidewalk. He was looking up and down the street, uncertain which way she had gone. Ari breathed a word of thanks that Rab had insisted on repainting her car. She stepped on the gas and sped through a yellow light.

Her hands and feet tingled with adrenaline, and it was several seconds before she realized that her shirt was wet. She plucked at it gingerly. Her fingertips reddened. Her shirt was soaked with blood!

CHAPTER
SIXTEEN

ARI'S STOMACH WAS HEAVING AND SHE FELT FAINT. *It could have been my own blood on the shirt. I walked into a nest of vampires!* Her fluorescent contact lenses burned painfully in her eyes, and the road ahead appeared to be an eerie lavender color.

She cast a nervous look behind her as she pulled over at a gas station. At least no one seemed to be following her. She popped the lenses out of her eyes and blinked rapidly in relief. The big yellow lights over the gas pumps, the gray expanse of oil-stained cement, everything seemed to have normal colors again. She slipped on her jacket to hide her bloodstained shirt. As she walked over to the attendant's booth, she noticed that her knees were weak.

Beside a stack of oil cans sat a lanky boy in khakis, his feet propped up on the dusty counter.

She saw that his cuticles were caked with oil, and she remembered with a shock the bony white fingers and glassy nails of the vampires, their gaunt faces and sunken cheeks. Horrible! Any one of them could have grabbed her as she ran out. Only now did she fully grasp the risk she had taken.

The washroom at the back of the lot smelled sour. Grime crunched under her shoes as she stepped in. In its corner stood a big trash bin overflowing with crumpled paper towels. A single bulb dangled from the cracked plaster ceiling. Ari stripped off her shirt and stood shivering as the water ran on the bloodstained cloth. The water ran pink into the dirty sink. The blood had probably spilled from some vampire's glass.

She wrung out the shirt and tried to scrub the white powder off her skin. Even after it was all gone, she was shockingly pale. The sight of Paul's face, towering above the crowd at the bar, haunted her. It was a face she loved. The voice that had called to her in the bar was as familiar as her own. But something about her twin's eyes was disturbingly different. Their glow was hard and inhuman.

Face it. She stared at her bleached face in the mirror. *You don't know him anymore. He's become someone else—someone who beats up his girlfriend, someone who kills. He wants to kill you.*

She leaned against the wall, feeling its cold

roughness between her shoulder blades. She knew she had to pull herself together. It was crucial that she be able to think straight, because Paul was clever and determined—and her life might depend on using her wits.

Ari drove away from the service station with her wet T-shirt wadded up on the seat beside her. The seams of the jacket she had put on rubbed against her bare skin. If only she had gotten a clearer idea of what Sophie had meant by Paul's "plan" to make her into a vampire. If only she hadn't panicked—she could have asked for details! Even some small clue might have told her what to do.

Suddenly all the steps she and Rab had taken to make themselves safe seemed inadequate and foolish—the unpublished phone number, the post office box taken in order to conceal their address, changing the license plate. What use were precautions as long as she had the chalice? It lay in her drawer, giving Paul a direct line to her. Maybe his plan was as simple as that—follow the signal of the chalice.

She knew she had been wrong to hide the chalice from Rab. After all his kindness to her, how could she possibly have justified putting him in unnecessary danger?

When she reached Charlottesville, she climbed the stairs of the apartment complex, glancing over her shoulder. But all she saw behind her was a bunch of kids carrying six-packs.

She slid her key in the lock, relieved that the

lights had been left on in the living room. Her nerves were on edge, and shadows made her jump. Rab must still be at the library. At least she wouldn't have to make a lot of awkward explanations. She tossed some necessities into a duffel bag—soap, jeans, underwear. Then she wrapped the chalice up in the underwear and zipped the bag shut.

Paul gazed up and down M Street, trying to spot someone with Ari's characteristic walk. His eyes strained, looking for a short cap of black curls bobbing in the crowd. But there was no sign of her. Tears of frustration stung his eyes.

As soon as he had stepped into the bar, he had known she was near. He had felt a soft twang, like a violin string that vibrates when the string next to it is plucked. Now that same intuitive feeling told him that she was gone.

He kicked himself for calling out her name. He should have waited until he was close enough to grab her. Maybe on some level he still hadn't quite grasped that she didn't want to see him. The look of terror on her face had been like cold water dashed in his face.

He turned and walked back into the dark bar. The loud music jangled his nerves, and the flash of the strobe light and the stink of blood made him nauseous. He slid onto the stool beside Sophie. "She's gone," he said dully. "I lost her."

An untouched glass sat on the counter, and several dollar bills lay folded beside it. Paul picked up one and sniffed it. Ari's smell lingered on it. The stool she had sat on was still warm.

Paul pressed his fingertips to his aching head. "How could I have let her get away?" he cried. "She was sitting right next to you. Did she say anything?"

Sophie gulped. "Only a few words."

"Did she ask about me?" he demanded

Sophie shook her head. "Really, she didn't say much."

"But she must have come here looking for me!" Paul pounded his fist on the bar and the glass of blood in front of him rattled. "Nothing else makes sense. But if she came here looking for me, why did she run away?" He felt a cool touch and spun around to face Verena.

She mocked him with her smile. "What's up, love? Why so glum?"

Paul forced himself to gulp down his anger. "I was hoping to get up with my sister, but I just missed her. That's all. It's no big deal."

Verena's eyes glowed softly like green opals. "I felt something a minute ago," she said. "I think she must have touched me. I even caught a whiff of human smell—" She wrinkled her nose. "I wish I had grabbed her then."

Paul saw the hunger in Verena's eyes. If she could have, she would have snatched Ari from him and made him watch while she sucked her dry.

"Verena," he said, with a coolness that surprised him, "would you step out back with me a minute?"

177

Her pink tongue skated over her lips. "Anytime, love." As she turned, she shot a sly look at Sophie.

"Paul, don't!" Sophie protested, grabbing his arm.

Paul gently removed her hand, then glanced over his shoulder at Verena. She was already turning toward the exit. He made a sudden decision and reached out as if to touch Sophie's cheek. But instead he slipped his hand past her ear, letting her wispy hair brush his fingers. He pressed his hand firmly to the back of her neck and, focusing his mind on her like a laser, he willed her to obey him.

He felt her shudder and suddenly she was staring at him with blank eyes. It had worked! She was in his power! Paul tried to conceal his excitement. He was afraid of breaking the spell. "I'm only going to talk to Verena, Sophie," he said in a careful monotone. "You stay here and wait for me."

"Yes, Paul." Her eyes did not shift. She looked straight ahead.

Pleased with himself, but feeling somehow vaguely unclean, Paul fled Sophie's blank gaze. He ran his finger around the inside of his shirt collar and straightened his chin purposefully. He was not a bit like his father, he assured himself. Desperate measures were needed just this once, but he didn't intend to make a habit of controlling Sophie. She would snap out of the trance soon enough.

Verena's eyes narrowed. "Don't think you can pull your tricks on me," she said. "I'll make you sorry if you even try." Prickles of uneasiness rose at the back of Paul's neck. He was afraid of Verena. She was not soft and compliant like Sophie. He knew all too well what it was like to squirm under her power. But he was desperate. Suddenly he pushed his way through the crowd, uncomfortably aware that he and Verena were drawing curious looks.

His sneakers crunched on gravel as he stepped into the alley. He closed the door behind them, muffling the loud music. Verena's metallic sequins caught stray light and shimmered as if they were the scales of a reptile. She drew her lip up and snarled.

"Why don't you pretend to be civilized for a change?" Paul folded his arms and stared at her distastefully.

"Why should I?" Her fangs flashed in a grin. "You love me the way I am."

Paul had the impulse to hit her, but he stifled it because he knew that in some weird way Verena got off on his hatred. Maybe she had been right when she said that his hate showed that she had power over him. One thing he was sure of—he could never defeat her by hitting her. He stared at her narrow face with its glimmering eyes, fascinated by the evil he saw there.

"Do you know what happened to my father?" Paul asked calmly.

Verena's smile faded. "I heard he had an accident."

"Somebody killed him with an incendiary bomb." Paul stared directly into her eyes, willing her with all his strength to believe him. "I know how to make an incendiary bomb, Verena. Did you realize that?"

"You killed him!" whispered Verena, stepping back. "You murdered your own father!"

"If you lay a hand on my sister, Verena, you're going to find out what fire tastes like."

She spat like a cat, with a snarling growl. "You only want Ari for yourself."

"You're right," said Paul. "I do."

"Your own sister! You're some kind of pervert."

Paul laughed. It was amusing to get a lecture on vampire mental health from Verena. "What do you care?" He smiled then and spread his arms over his head suddenly. "Boom!"

"Keep away from me." Verena whimpered.

"No, come here!" Paul stepped toward her. "We're a lot alike, you know that? I'd get a special kick out of—"

But Verena had vanished into the darkness.

Paul stood in the alley for several moments, grinning. Then he slipped back inside.

When he got back to Sophie he saw that she hadn't moved since he had left her. She sat stiffly on the bar stool, her hands folded primly in her lap.

He shook her a little and was relieved to see

the light flicker in her eyes. She blinked at him, as if she were waking up.

"Aren't you going to ask me what Verena and I were doing?" he teased.

She shook her head.

Paul grinned. "I've been scaring her witless, that's all. She's not so tough when you know how to handle her." Paul buried his face against Sophie's shoulder and laughed. The look on Verena's face! It had been priceless.

Sophie pulled away from him. "I don't want you to see her anymore." She looked down, avoiding his eyes, and fiddled with the loose ring on her finger.

Paul gasped with laughter. "No problem! Honestly! I promise."

Suddenly Paul caught a glimpse of himself in the mirror and his heart twisted inside him. Ari's hair looked like his now that it was short. Twins. They belonged together. "Sophie," he said suddenly, "did my sister know who you were? I mean, did she realize that you're my girl-friend?"

"I don't know. How could I know, Paul?" She slid off the stool. "I think I'd better go. I'm tired."

Paul got up. "I'll go with you. Let's go out the other way." He jerked his head toward the back entrance. As he guided Sophie, dodging sharp elbows, he was thoughtful. "I guess you couldn't possibly have known she was my sister."

"Oh, I didn't!" cried Sophie. "I thought at

first she was one of us—a vampire, you know."

Paul pushed the back door open and let it swing shut behind them. Overhead, he could make out a thin strip of the luminous city sky above the alley. He had developed an affection for this stinking little alley. It was, after all, the scene of his triumph over Verena. "If you didn't know it was Ari," he said, "you might have talked pretty openly, huh? I know how sometimes you tell strangers things you wouldn't tell your best friend. Like people you sit next to on a plane or a bus and you know you'll never see them again. You can end up spilling a lot. We'd had a big fight and you were upset. You must have cried. Did you tell Ari your troubles, Sophie?"

Sophie's blue eyes were wide with fear, and Paul knew it would be easy to shake the truth out of her.

"Did you tell her about me?" asked Paul. "Did you tell her I hit you? Like this?" Suddenly he slapped Sophie so hard the blow echoed at the end of the alley. He heard her head knock against the brick wall.

"I didn't know who she was!" sobbed Sophie.

"Tell me the truth and I won't hit you again," said Paul. "The truth, now, remember! Did you tell her I was going to make her into a vampire!"

"I didn't know who she was, Paul! Or I never would have."

"You *did* tell her!" he cried. "Why'd you do that?" He grabbed her and shook her. She twisted out of his grasp and stared at him. He banged his fist on the wall. "It was so stupid!" he cried. "Now she'll never let me near her!"

"I'm sorry," whimpered Sophie. "I'm so sorry."

"She came here looking for me! She wanted me! Tomorrow we could have been walking hand in hand under the stars, sharing everything, telling each other all our secrets!" He choked on a sob. "I could have taught her everything I know. You ruined that, Sophie! You ruined it for me."

"I didn't mean to," she whispered.

Paul's eyes were blurred with tears, and Sophie's face looked to him as if it were melting. "It's hopeless." He choked. "I'll never find her."

"It'll be all right. You'll think of something," said Sophie.

A cold ache gripped his gut when he heard the pity in her voice. What was he doing slapping Sophie around, he wondered, when she was the only friend he had left in the world? "I'm sorry I hit you," he choked. "I'm rotten. No wonder Ari's afraid of me. Look at me. I'm such a jerk."

He felt Sophie's hand touch his cheek. "It's okay, Paul," she said. "Really. I know you only hit me because you're upset."

He tried to smile. "You could hit me back. I would let you."

She shook her head. "I'm not like Verena."

He heard the edge to her voice, and he

smiled through his tears. "You don't have to worry about her. We're finished. I've taken care of that, and she's not going to bother us anymore."

Sophie's eyes widened. "What did you do to her, Paul?"

"Just scared her off, that's all."

They walked together to Sophie's car. She had parked on M Street, and it hurt Paul to walk past the very spot that he had somehow let Ari slip from his grasp. He gazed up at an indifferent sky, thinking of how Ari was gone and how he might never see her again.

The sound of Sophie's motor starting up startled him out of his black thoughts, and he bent to look in her car window. Her face was hard to read, but he suspected she was still mad at him for being mean to her. "You are going home, aren't you?" he asked anxiously.

She shook her head. "Not yet."

Paul wondered if Sophie was going to go find Dubay to cry on his shoulder. And worse. He thrust his hands into his pockets, afraid he couldn't stop himself from hitting her. "Okay. That's cool," he choked. "Do whatever you want to do. But I promise things are going to be better between us, Sophie. I'm serious."

She didn't answer, and he watched as her car drove off. At least she hadn't given him back his ring, he thought. That must mean something.

*   *   *

184

Ari glanced around at the dark buildings of St. Anselm's and listened to the wind whispering through the bare trees. She still wasn't sure what had brought her here to her old school.

On the long drive back to town, she had told herself over and over that she had to get rid of the chalice. Yet somehow she hadn't been able to bring herself to leave it alongside the road. She had thought about pitching it in a river, but then she had crossed the Potomac without stopping. She supposed she must not want to destroy the chalice after all. Actions, after all, spoke louder than words. She only wanted to tuck it away for safekeeping. She had brought the chalice here, to a place that had once been safe and familiar.

Tonight, however, the St. Anselm's campus did not seem either safe or familiar. It breathed danger, as if it had somehow been infected by her own fear. The few lights that burned low around the stone buildings cast long, eerie shadows. Overhead, voices hissed at her from bare branches, calling her name: *"Ar—ee."*

She glanced up fearfully and saw glowing spots in the trees, small and intense like hundreds of tiny lights. There was a sudden movement, and she saw a fuzzy outline and a pair of pointed ears silhouetted against the sky. "You'll be sorry," the creature whined. "Sorry, very sor-ry."

The words faded into the wind. To Ari's astonishment the chalice clung to her fingers as if held by suction. She tried to shake it off and stared down at it, aghast. Her fingers were sticking to the gold! Her hands tingled. Was it possible the gold wouldn't let her go? Was she doomed to keep it forever?

She closed her eyes. "This is ridiculous," she said aloud, oddly reassured by the firmness of her voice. "A stupid gold cup can't tell me what to do." She peeled her fingers off the chalice, and to her relief it fell with a clang to the cement walk. She kicked it behind a shrub. Then she turned and ran.

CHAPTER SEVENTEEN

PAUL'S SHOULDERS SLUMPED AS HE WALKED DOWN M Street. Nagging at his mind was the possibility that the gold might hold some key to help him find Ari. Some line of sympathy seemed to run between the two chalices—some strong signal. There had to be some way he could use that to find her.

But he was afraid. Tonight the gold had driven him almost insane with jealousy. He had come close to losing Sophie—he might lose her yet if he were not careful. No, using the gold to find Ari was too risky.

He understood now why his aunt had kept it hidden away. Its magic was double-edged, both beneficial and dangerous. There was something infernal about the way it reflected and magnified his darkest fears. Even now, the memory of the sick jealousy he had felt made him squirm uneasily. The gold nourished the darkness inside him, and he couldn't risk putting himself in its power again. But how else could he find Ari?

Paul looked up and saw he had almost reached the grocery store on the corner of M Street and Wisconsin. A red-haired girl bounced out its door carrying a bag of groceries. She was too far away for him to see her face, but from the vivid color of her hair, Paul had no doubt about who it was. "Sybil!" he called.

She turned and waved her arm enthusiastically. Moments before, he had been sunk in despair; now he was breathless with hope. He ran and threw his arms around her, squeezing her tight, groceries and all. Her face was fiery with self-consciousness.

"It's so great to see you!" Paul cried.

"I-it's nice to see you again, Paul, too," she stuttered. "We've really missed you at school."

I'll bet. Half the school had come to his house in a mob to try to kill him—but he pretended to take the remark in the friendly spirit she had intended. He beamed down at her, careful to hide his fangs. "It's been so long since I've seen you! I guess you haven't even seen my new car."

"You've got a new car?"

"Yeah, want to take a spin in it? It's really something."

"I don't know." She hesitated. "I've got all these groceries. I ought to get them home."

"We can put them in your car. We won't be gone long."

"Okay." She smiled.

Paul helped her put the groceries in her car.

"Where are you parked?" she asked.

"About a block from here. I don't like to park on the main street. You know how it is when you've got a new car—you worry all the time about getting dents and scratches."

Paul was grateful for the dim light and the shadows that crisscrossed the sidewalk as they made their way to his car. Sybil had never shown any fear of him, but there was no sense pushing his luck. She must know that the kids at school thought he was a vampire. If she got a good look at him . . .

Paul thrust his hands deep in his pockets to hide his glassy fingernails. "You know, since Rab and Ari moved," he said, "I've done the stupidest thing—I lost their address! I can't even call, because the number is unlisted. Ari left a message on my machine, and she's probably wondering why I haven't called back."

"I'm afraid I can't help you out," said Sybil, glancing up at him. "Rab didn't give me the new number."

Paul stopped walking suddenly. "Your own brother didn't give you his new phone number?"

Sybil made a face. "I guess Mom and Dad told him not to. They have it—but they're all acting like I'm such a big mouth, because I let Cos

189

know you two were still alive. Now nobody tells me anything."

Paul's disappointment felt like a blow to his stomach. They had reached the Jaguar, but for once the sight of it brought him no pleasure.

"Is this your car?" cried Sybil, running her finger lightly along the sleek black finish. "Cool!"

"Yeah," said Paul abruptly. "Get in." He could taste his bitter anger. The Barrons knew where Ari was, but they wouldn't tell him! His own sister—and he couldn't even get her phone number! Rage swelled in him as he slid in behind the wheel. Suddenly he became conscious of Sybil's eyes on him, and his face lit up with a careful smile.

"It's so cold out." Sybil shivered as he pulled out of his parking place. "Look how our breath is fogging up the windows."

Paul's breath never fogged the windows these days. It was Sybil's breath, but he switched on the defogger.

"Did you hear about Jessie's car crash?" Sybil asked, rubbing her hands together.

"No." Paul's head snapped around. "Is he okay?"

"No! He was killed! Isn't that terrible? People are starting to make awful jokes about all the kids at school who have d—" Sybil stopped abruptly, realizing probably that the choice of subject wasn't tactful. "I hate black humor," she said. "Anyway, since it happened,

190

I've gotten so nervous about driving, you wouldn't believe."

Sybil wriggled out of her parka and tossed it in the backseat. Now that her jacket was off, Paul watched her with fascination. The hollow at the base of her neck deepened slightly and then grew shallower as she breathed. She was talking about how she had only barely passed the driving test, but Paul wasn't listening.

Sybil's family held the secret to Ari's whereabouts. And now he had Sybil. He smiled. Maybe some kind of trade could be arranged. "Want to see where I live?" he asked.

Sybil glanced at him in surprise. "Yeah, but how would your dad feel about your bringing guests home this late?"

"Oh, he's—" Paul decided suddenly it might not be a good idea to mention his father's death. Even Sybil might get suspicious when she noticed that virtually everyone he knew was dead. "He's not around tonight," Paul finished.

"Is it some woman?" asked Sybil, sympathetically. "Ari told me your dad was kind of wild."

Paul smiled. In a way it was a woman who was responsible for his father's absence. "Yes," he said. "Some woman."

"Do you like her?" asked Sybil.

"Yeah, I like her. But I don't really see that much of her."

"So where are you living now?" Sybil polished a clear spot on the window and peered outside. "Is it far from here?"

191

"You'll never guess." He smiled. "Right across from St. Anselm's!"

"Get out of here!" exclaimed Sybil. "You're not serious."

"Dead serious." Paul smiled.

"But—isn't that taking kind of a risk?" Sybil blinked. "I mean, weren't a lot of our class-mates—"

"Trying to kill me?" Paul finished for her.

She nodded, suddenly embarrassed.

"You can't go on living if you're afraid of every shadow." Paul shrugged. "I know Ari was real spooked, but I decided I had to put all that stuff behind me and get on with my life." He parked the car in front of the apartment build-ing.

Sybil gazed at the building curiously. "I never even noticed there were apartments here. Isn't it weird to think you've been able to look out and see us and we've never even known you were here? Of course, I guess mostly you're in school when we're on campus. Where are you going to school now?"

"The Friends School," lied Paul. "A Quaker school appealed to me. You know—peace, broth-erhood."

Sybil smiled suddenly. "A change from St. Anselm's, huh?" she suggested.

"You said it."

Sybil reached for the door handle.

"Wait a minute." Paul touched her. "Why don't we just sit out here awhile."

Sybil turned pink as she turned toward him. "You mean and talk some more?"

"Yeah," said Paul softly. He drew her close, then brushed his lips against the bare skin at the base of her neck. She was warm, and he could sense the blood pulsing under her soft flesh.

"That tickles." She giggled.

Suddenly he opened his mouth and bit her hard. He heard her gasp with pain and felt the tremor of her body as he dug his teeth deeper into her flesh. The blood that gushed suddenly into his mouth almost robbed him of his senses.

Stop! screamed a voice in his head. Shuddering, he pushed himself away from her and pressed his fingers firmly against her flesh. Sybil's mouth had fallen open, and her eyes were closed, but to Paul's relief, he could feel a ragged pulse of blood under his fingers. She was alive.

He leapt out of the car and gave a swift glance up and down the sidewalk to make sure no one was coming. Then he opened the car door, unfastened her seat belt, and pulled her out. Luckily there was still no sign of anyone.

He carried her cradled in his arms. Balancing her carefully on one knee, he managed to open the door to the fire stairs.

She was not heavy, but Paul felt the unaccustomed strain in his legs as he mounted the flights of stairs. It worried him a little that her breathing seemed uneven. Maybe he had overdone it with her blood. He had only intended to send her into unconsciousness, but he knew it was easy to lose track of what was going on in the heat of the moment.

He was surprised to find that he was breathless by the time he had reached the second landing. Nerves, he guessed. But as long as he didn't meet somebody walking down the fire stairs, he should be okay. And he wasn't likely to run into anybody. Most of the tenants in the apartment building used the elevator.

By the time they reached the fourth floor, Sybil was stirring, making a low moan. Paul paused to press his fingers against her neck. "Sybil, go to sleep!" he commanded.

Her eyelids fluttered uncertainly. Paul was unsure whether his trick would work on someone who was unconscious. She couldn't hear him or feel his touch, so maybe not. He wasn't sure whether it was possible to hypnotize an unconscious person.

He nudged open the fire door with his foot and peeked out, relieved to see that no one was in the hall. Shoving the door open, he staggered to his apartment. Sybil's color wasn't good, and he was anxious to take her pulse.

Suddenly the door swung open. "Paul!" Sophie cried. "What's going on?" Her alarmed glance rested on the unconscious girl.

Paul stepped in at once and kicked the door closed behind him. "Let's tie her up and gag her. She may be coming to." He laid Sybil down on the couch.

Sophie wrung her hands. "But who *is* she? What are you doing? Are you insane, bringing her here?"

"I had to. Now help me!"

Paul tore a sash from the curtains, forced it between Sybil's teeth, then lifted her head up and tied it behind her head. It was hard to know exactly how tight it should be. He couldn't risk having her scream and rouse the building—but on the other hand he didn't want her to choke to death, either. He ripped the other curtain sash down. The ruffled curtains fell straight to the floor, obscuring the narrow balcony outside.

Paul pressed his fingers to the inside of Sybil's wrist to check her pulse. Ragged, he judged, but reasonably strong. Then he tied her wrists together behind her back. "Do we have any more of these curtain things?" he asked. "I'd better tie her feet, too. I don't want her running off."

"No, but just a minute. I've got some panty hose," said Sophie. She ran into the bedroom, and Paul could hear her rummaging in her bureau. She returned with a handful of limp brown nylon.

Paul stretched them out. "You *wear* those things?" he asked in amazement. "Jeez, they look uncomfortable." He flexed them between his hands, pleased to see they would make a strong and flexible bond. He tied Sybil's ankles together, knotting the legs of the panty hose.

"Paul, who is she?" Sophie protested. "Will you please explain to me what is going on?"

Suddenly Sybil's eyes flew open, and she regarded them with horror. Paul was pleased to see that she was breathing pretty normally and her color looked better. "She's my little bargaining chip," he said smiling. "Sybil is her name. Not that her name matters. What matters is that she's Ari's best friend. And get this—Sybil's folks know where Ari is."

"So you're going to make them tell you?" asked Sophie. "But is it a good idea to go about it this way, Paul? Won't it upset Ari more when she finds out what you've done?"

"It doesn't matter. I'm not waiting for Ari to come to me this time. Sybil's folks are going to deliver her." Paul smiled and reached for the phone. He swiftly punched in the Barrons' number.

A sleepy-sounding male voice answered.

Paul glanced at his watch. "It's eleven-fifteen," he said smoothly. "Do you know where your daughter is?"

"Who is this?" cried Mr. Barron, alarmed.

"It's Paul Montclair, Mr. Barron. I've got Sybil and she's okay. But if you want to get her back alive, make sure my sister is delivered to my apartment by dawn. As soon as I've got Ari, I'll tell you where Sybil is. But remember, if anything happens to me, you'll never find Sybil."

"Let me speak to her!" demanded Mr. Barron.

"Sure." Paul handed the receiver to Sophie.

"Put the phone near her mouth, Sophie. I'm going to ungag her just for a second. Okay, Sybil, tell your dad that you're okay."

Paul unknotted the gag.

"I'm near St. Anselm's, Daddy," cried Sybil. Paul snapped the gag back in her mouth and pulled it so tight she gasped with the pain.

After a minute he loosened it. "Get something to stuff in her mouth, Sophie," he growled. "She could chew right through this thing if we're not careful."

Sophie dashed back into the bedroom.

Paul picked up the phone. "As you can tell, Mr. Barron, Sybil is her usual lively self. I know you want to get her back in that same undamaged condition. *So bring Ari to me.*" Machine-gun style, he rattled off the address of the apartment. "And don't think you're going to find Sybil without me, because I'm moving her right now. You don't have much time." Paul hung up. "Her dad was about to pass out, he was so scared," he said. "I think we're going to get results."

"But Paul, don't you see?" Sophie cried. "He can't make Ari come to you. What if she refuses?"

"She won't," he said. "Sybil's her best friend. You think she wants Sybil's death on her conscience?"

Sybil's frightened eyes were darting about as if she were looking for clues to how to get away.

"Where are you going to hide her?" asked

Sophie. "They could be here any minute."

"Don't worry. I've got it all figured out," said Paul. "I only brought her up here so she could talk to her dad and prove that I had her." She squirmed desperately as he lifted her into his arms. "Sybil, stop it," snapped Paul, "or I'll have to knock you out again."

Sybil's eyes widened and she became still. Sophie opened the door for them. As Paul carried Sybil out, he was alarmed to hear the click of an opening door down the hall. Swearing under his breath, he ran for the fire stairs. Sybil struggled so desperately that he almost dropped her. Still, somehow he managed to get into the stairwell and close the door behind him before anyone saw them.

He stood on the landing, trying to catch his breath. Suddenly he felt a sharp blow on his nose. Sybil's bent knees had hit him. She straightened out suddenly, and Paul overbalanced and almost fell downstairs.

Furious, he dumped her on the concrete landing. He heard her head hit the floor, but the fall didn't knock her out. She still squirmed frantically. He bent over her and leaned his weight on her, pinning her shoulders against the cement. He could tell by the way she shuddered that he had scared her. He spoke softly but with an edge to his voice. "Sybil, I've already murdered Susannah, and Nadia, and Jessie." He saw the whites of her eyes as she stared at him in horror. "Yes, Jessie." He smiled. "I dragged the

198

stupid jerk out of his car and finished him off. So don't believe for a minute that I'd hesitate to kill you."

He could feel that her entire body was rigid. It was amazing how expressive a person could be, Paul thought, even when trussed up like a turkey.

"You've already served your purpose," Paul said. "Now it doesn't much matter what happens to you. They're going to bring Ari to me just the same. The only reason I'm bothering to keep you alive is as a kind of insurance policy." He smiled. "But if you make a big pain of yourself, I won't bother. So keep still if you know what's good for you."

Paul could see the rising and falling of her chest as she panted for breath. With a grunt, Paul hoisted her awkwardly over his shoulder. This time she made no more effort to squirm out of his grasp.

When he reached the foot of the stairs, Paul put her down again and darted outside to make sure the coast was clear. Luckily he and Sophie lived in a quiet neighborhood. Nothing was stirring. A low mist hung just above the street.

Paul unlocked the trunk of the car, then went back to get Sybil.

As soon as he opened the door to the fire stairs, he realized she had been squirming wildly while he was gone. Her face was shiny with sweat, and the damp moisture had made her red hair stand out from her head as if it were electrified. Her frightened eyes followed him as he bent over her.

He was intrigued by her gaze—it was so unlike the crystalline brilliance of vampire eyes. She was so warm and alive, so determined against the odds to stay alive, that she stirred in him an uncomfortable envy, and he felt the familiar deep longing—he wanted her life, her breath, everything human. Suddenly he sank to his knees. "Sybil," he murmured, "have you ever had a date with a vampire?"

She quivered and recoiled when he touched cold fingers to her cheek, turning her head away from him.

"I always got the idea you liked me, Sybil," he whispered. "What's the problem all of a sudden? All I want to do is to suck everything human right out of your beautiful little body and make it all mine."

She struggled as he grabbed her, but he pressed the heel of his hand against her cheek, forcing her head to the side to expose the luscious curve of her throat. Then he sank his teeth deep into the flesh. Blood filled his mouth to overflowing and spilled out the corners of his lips. The unformed feeling had come to him as he drank that killing Sybil would hurt Ari. He remembered how sad Ari had looked on the day of their mother's funeral. What was he doing? He couldn't kill Sybil and make her sad again. He pushed his hand suddenly in front of his mouth and forced himself away from the rushing blood.

His heart was beating so hard he was dizzy, and he passed his hand down his face in confusion and dismay. He pressed his fist to his open mouth, feeling his fangs cut against his own flesh as he tried to collect his thoughts. He was scarcely even aware that his other hand was pressed against Sybil's throat, stemming the flow of blood, sealing the torn flesh. Suddenly alarmed, he ripped open Sybil's shirt and placed his palm flat against her chest. To his relief he could feel the thud of her heart. She was still alive.

He lifted her suddenly in his arms and hurried out to the car, afraid he would change his mind. He dumped her in the trunk. The car rocked with her sudden weight. He slammed the trunk closed, and without looking back he dashed back into the building.

As he ran upstairs, he was vaguely aware that since Sybil had lost blood, she must be both dehydrated and weak. He could get her something to drink, he thought. But then he realized that it was a bad idea to force liquids down somebody who was unconscious.

Mr. Barron better not take long getting hold of Ari, he thought grimly. *Sybil might not make it.*

CHAPTER
EIGHTEEN

THE PHONE BESIDE COS'S BED BURST FORTH WITH A
loud ring. Cos's eyes flew open, and he grabbed
for it. It fell off the bedside table with a disso-
nant clang. By the time he fished up the dangling receiver by its cord, he could hear his
father's agitated voice on the line.

"Hullo?"

"May I speak to Cos, please?" said Rab's
voice.

"Young man!" Cos's dad exploded. "Do you
have any idea what time it is?"

"I'm sorry, sir," said Rab. "But this is an
emergency."

"I've got it, Dad," Cos said at once. His father hung up. "What's wrong, Rab?" he asked
anxiously. "Is Ari okay?"

"I thought you could tell me! You haven't
seen her?" Rab's voice was desperate. "Damn. I

thought she would have gone to you when she left here."

Cos sat up in bed, shivering. He pulled the covers around his shoulders. "What's happened? Fill me in. Maybe I can help."

"I don't see what you can do to help unless you know where Ari is," cried Rab.

"Have you tried over at Sybil's?"

"Cos, he's *got* Sybil!"

"*Who's* got Sybil?" Cos inquired cautiously.

"Paul! He's kidnapped Sybil, and he says he won't tell us where he's hidden her unless we hand over Ari."

"You can't give him Ari!" Cos whispered, appalled.

"I thought she might be able to reason with him, at least. But it's no good. Paul seems convinced we've got Ari, but we don't. And if you don't know where she is, then I guess nobody does."

"When did she leave your place?" said Cos, holding the phone against his shoulder with his chin. Already he was reaching for the jeans that lay in a heap on the floor beside his bed.

"I'm not sure. Sometime this evening. When I got home from the library, all I found was a note on the fridge saying that it'd be better for me if she took off."

"No clue about where she'd gone?"

"Not one. I've turned the apartment upside down looking for some kind of lead."

"Did you find anything?"

"My sleeping bag is missing."

"Your sleeping bag is missing," Cos repeated numbly. "Jeez, that could mean anything. She could be at a beach, a highway rest stop, sleeping in the car—anyplace in the world."

"She's probably not sleeping outside in this weather," said Rab.

Cos hoped he was right. The idea of Ari bunking at some highway rest stop scared the heck out of him.

"Dad's called the cops and the FBI," Rab said. "They're throwing a net around Paul's apartment right this minute. Maybe they'll find where he's hidden Sybil. I don't see how he could have gotten too far with her."

"Where does he live?" asked Cos.

Rab laughed shortly. "Right across the street from St. Anselm's. Can you believe that? Right under our noses. Look, if you hear from Ari or if you have any idea where she might be, I mean *any* idea, call my parents' place. We're all going to be standing by until we find Sybil." His voice broke suddenly.

Cos was too kindhearted to point out that there was a good chance Sybil was already dead. Susannah. Nadia. Jessie. If Paul had murdered all three of them, why would he stop there? Poor Sybil. The thought that she might be lying cold and dead somewhere made him sick to his stomach.

Already adrenaline was surging through his sleepy body. As soon as he hung up the phone, he pulled on a sweatshirt and jerked a parka out of his closet. About all he could hope for now was that he could somehow save Ari. He tied his shoes and pocketed his car keys.

He tiptoed out his bedroom door, relieved that the house was silent. His parents had gone back to sleep. The only noise was the faint rumble of the refrigerator. He scrawled a note for his parents in case he didn't get back by morning.

Outside, a gentle mist rose from the grass. The sky was so overcast that the stars had disappeared. He leaned against his car and closed his eyes, feeling the cold, damp air against his face. Now that he was out of the house, he realized that his instinct for action had gotten ahead of him. He had no clear idea of what to do next. He could join the crowd that he figured was forming outside Paul's apartment—but that didn't seem too smart.

If he were Ari and he were really scared on a night like this, where would he go?

Sophie peered out the window. "Paul, I think something's going on down on the street."

Mist obscured what was going on below, but Paul could tell that more vehicles were parked on the street than usual. He caught a glimpse of some dark figures moving quickly.

Paul turned away from the window. Just then he heard a distant knock. It sounded as if it came from down the hall. He threw an alarmed glance at Sophie. Going to the front door, he pressed his ear against it and heard the low murmur of voices outside. They weren't close—maybe they were by the elevator. He couldn't tell how many were out there.

"Sybil's folks must have called the cops," said Sophie.

Paul swore. "Why'd they have to do that? All they need to do is send Ari up here, and I'd have let Sybil go."

Sophie peered anxiously out the window. "What are we going to do, Paul?"

"You don't have to stay here. The cops don't have anything on you. Just go. You ought to get away with no trouble."

She clung to him. "I don't want to leave without you."

Paul knew he should urge her to leave, but somehow he couldn't. When he pressed his ear to the door, he heard the elevator going down. He drew away and gazed bleakly at Sophie. "I think they must be evacuating the building. That's probably why people are out in the hall."

"What do you think that means?" Sophie's eyes glowed and shifted uneasily.

Paul shrugged. "Maybe they're planning a shoot-out. Maybe they're going to throw tear bombs through the window."

"Bullets and tear gas wouldn't hurt us."

Paul grinned. "You're right. How can we lose? We're already dead—technically. And I can't see them setting the entire building on fire. When it comes right down to it, all they can do is grab us and carry us away to jail."

"I don't want to be grabbed and put in jail," whimpered Sophie.

"Don't worry." He frowned. "We'll get away. I'll think of something."

Sophie gazed apprehensively out the window. "There are a lot of them out there, Paul."

Paul was sure that he and Sophie could do a lot of damage if the police came rushing at them. Police blood would flow like a river. But Sophie was not a fighter, and he didn't want to put her through a bloody confrontation with cops when they were so heavily outnumbered.

The phone rang and Paul snatched at it, his heart racing.

"This is Ben Harris from the police mediation team," said a voice. "I want to let you know that the block is surrounded. We'd like to give you an opportunity to come out peacefully."

Yeah, I'd bet you'd like for me to come out peacefully.

"Would you like some sandwiches or something?" Harris went on. "Or is there someone you'd like to talk to?"

"My sister!" Paul yelled. "Get me my sister." He slammed the receiver down.

The phone at once rang again. Paul picked it up. "I told you—" he began.

"This is Hilda Acre of the *Washington Post*," said an earnest young voice.

"No comment!" yelled Paul, slamming the re-

208

ceiver down. "Can you believe it? It's the newspaper! They're all a bunch of ghouls. . . ." He ran to the window. "What is going on down there?" He could make out flashing blue lights in the fog, and he had the sensation of movement. Of course, if the police were really evacuating the apartment building, that meant a lot of people would be out on the street. "Where is Ari?" he cried. "Why hasn't she come?"

Ari snuggled into her sleeping bag. The darkness around her was complete. It was as if she were deep in a cave. She wished she had thought to bring a candle, or even a flashlight—but darkness had its advantages. She was securely hidden. Paul didn't even know this cabin existed. Now that she had rid herself of the chalice, there was no way he could find her.

Ari had stuffed her wallet with large bills before leaving Rab's apartment, and she knew that amount of money would carry her a long way. When light broke she would think about what to do next. She had a car, and it was a big enough country in which to disappear—forever.

Rab must have found her note by now. Later she would write him a letter and explain.

Rab sat miserably on his parents' living room couch, staring at the family portrait framed in silver. Sybil had still had her braces on when it was taken. "I'll never forgive myself—" he began.

"Rab, would you stop saying that!" snapped

209

Mr. Barron. "There's no reason for us to expect the worst, none at all. Sybil was very much alive when I spoke to her, and at this minute the top law enforcement men in the nation are on the case. I've talked to Cliff Eagleton, and he says, if necessary in this sort of case they can do a house-to-house search of the entire area. They'll pull out all the stops. Besides, the boy couldn't have taken her far in the time he had after I hung up. She must be close by, and in a town this thickly populated somebody's bound to have seen or heard something." He clenched his fists. "We'll get her back."

The doorbell rang, and Mr. Barron kicked over the wastebasket in his sudden rush to get to the door. Wastepaper was flung all over the Oriental rug, but neither he nor Rab stopped to pick it up. Mr. Barron jerked the door open.

Mr. Barron's law partner stood on the stoop, bundled up in a coat and muffler. The man's wife, with her streaked hair pulled into a bun, stood a half-step behind him. Her head was drawn down into the collar of her fur coat and she was shivering.

"Any news?" barked Eagleton.

Mr. Barron shook his head miserably.

"How is Anne?" His partner hung his coat in the coat closet.

"The doctor just left her," croaked Mr. Barron, running a hand over his thinning hair. "He gave her such a heavy sedative that I don't think she even knows what's going on, bless her.

I hope by the time she comes out of it, Sybil will be home."

The shifting of the Eagletons' eyes told Rab that they did not share his father's optimism. He felt suddenly furious at them. But no—he shouldn't direct his anger at them. Everything that had happened was his fault. He had gotten Sybil into this, because of his stupid desire to know his "blood" relatives. Rab winced at the thought.

Mrs. Eagleton peeled off her gloves. "Where is Anne, darling? I want to go to her."

Rab led her up the stairs to his mother's darkened room. Even before they reached the door to the bedroom, he could hear her muttering. It obviously wasn't true that she didn't know what was going on. The doctor's sedative had only plunged her into a deeper nightmare.

Rab tiptoed into the room.

"Blood!" cried his mother suddenly, throwing her arms out spread-eagle on the bed.

Mrs. Eagleton pulled up a chair by the bed and took the unconscious woman's hand in hers. Rab felt a rush of gratitude for her kindness. "It's going to be all right, darling," she murmured softly. "We're looking for Sybil right now. Everything's going to be fine."

His mother muttered something incoherent. Rab felt he could no longer stand seeing her blank staring eyes and the jerking muscles that made her mouth seem out of control. "Do you

211

think you can manage here, Mrs. Eagleton?" he asked abruptly.

"I'll stay right here and not budge. Don't worry—I won't leave her alone."

Rab fled.

When he got downstairs, he found the other two men standing in the living room with their heads close together, talking. They looked up, and Rab had the feeling they had been talking about him. "I'm going over to Paul's apartment," Rab said suddenly. "I don't want to stay here all night, waiting for the phone to ring. If I do I'll go crazy."

Cliff Eagleton laid a hand on his friend's shoulder. "You go, too, if you like. Betty and I can hold the fort here."

Rab watched as his father scrawled a name and number on a memo pad. "Here's the police contact person," Mr. Barron said, "in case you need to get through to me."

Rab and his father were out of the house in seconds. They ran the light at the corner of Dunbarton and then sped toward St. Anselm's.

"Cos promised he'd call the house if he heard anything," said Rab.

"Do you have any idea why Ari took off so suddenly?" asked Mr. Barron. "It seems very peculiar that she left just before this happened . . ." His voice trailed off.

"I wonder if Paul threatened her somehow." Rab drummed his fingers on the dashboard.

"How could he possibly threaten her? I

thought she had made a clean break from him and they weren't even in contact with each other."

"I don't know." Rab bit his lip. "Sometimes I had the feeling she wasn't telling me the whole truth."

Ari was awakened by the low rumble of a motor. It was drawing closer, she realized, and she abruptly sat up in the darkness. Her heart began pounding. Suddenly the motor stopped, and she felt herself go cold. She had broken in—so the door was unlocked.

Perhaps it's only a neighbor, she thought, her mind racing—a neighbor who had heard her car go by on the road and had come to check on things. But when Ari heard footsteps outside, she knew with grim certainty that a neighbor wouldn't come out in the middle of the night to check on an empty cabin.

She heard the soft brushing sound of sneaker soles on the cement steps outside. Then the door creaked open, and a beam of light played on the rough surface of the wall. The light found the black hole of the fireplace next, and then shone on a broom that stood in the corner.

Ari froze. She could hear heavy breathing near the door. Then she heard a footfall, and the cabin floor creaked. She cringed, hoping that somehow the beam of light would miss her and the intruder would go away. But the beam was moving methodically back and forth from wall to wall. It was as if the intruder had mentally graphed the floor and was checking every inch.

Ari slid out of the sleeping bag and lunged forward, making a frantic dash for the door. In her panic she ran up against the intruder and his flashlight fell. She heard a hoarse yell behind her as she stumbled barefoot down the steps. Her car was close by, and she leapt into it, locking the door with trembling fingers. She turned on the lights.

Cos stood before her, his arm thrown up to shield his eyes from the glare. "Cos!" Ari shrieked. "You scared the hell out of me! You're lucky I didn't die of a heart attack!" She got out of the car.

"Ari, it's so good to see you," he said hoarsely, reaching out. "What happened to your hair?"

"I cut it." She threw herself into his arms and sobbed. "Why didn't you let me know it was you? You scared me to death." She pounded her fist against his chest.

He laughed. "You used to drive a different car. I thought . . . well . . . maybe some drug dealer had started using the place or something."

Ari sniffled. "No, actually, this is my car. It's just been painted. Wait a minute, let me get my shoes and jacket from in there. My feet are freezing." She gingerly picked her way back to the cabin and retrieved her shoes and socks. She slid into a jacket and sat on the steps. The glaring light of the headlights was shining on her. She lifted a hand to shade her eyes and looked at Cos with puzzlement. "But what are you *doing* out here in the middle of the night, Cos?"

"Rab called me and said you'd come up missing."

"He didn't know where I'd gone," said Ari promptly. "I didn't tell anybody."

"I played a wild hunch. I remembered when we'd been out here camping. The place seemed like it was a million miles from civilization, though it's not that far from town, really. So it hit me you might come here if you wanted a place to hide."

She shivered. "Couldn't you have waited until tomorrow to visit? I wish I could tell you how creepy it was to hear your footsteps."

"It's an emergency, Ari," Cos said somberly. "Paul's kidnapped Sybil, and he wants to trade her for you."

Ari felt as if all the blood in her body had been replaced with ice. With a single sentence, Cos had told her that her life was over.

When she spoke, it felt as if her mouth belonged to someone else. "Oh. Well, I guess I'll have to go to him."

"Don't be stupid." Cos grabbed her arm to keep her from getting back in the car. "Chances are he's already killed Sybil."

She shook her head. "He wouldn't do that! He only wants me. I'll go to him."

"Oh, no, you don't." Cos snatched the keys out of the ignition and slipped them into his coat pocket.

"Give me those!" cried Ari. "You can't stop me!"

Cos thought about it. "I bet I can," he stated. "I'm bigger, heavier, and probably a little bit more determined."

Ari sagged against the car and wept.

"Come on," Cos said gently. He gathered her into his arms, and she gasped at the sudden comfort she felt at his touch. "It's not that bad," he murmured. "Maybe Sybil's okay. Maybe you can reason with him."

Ari nodded. She knew Cos was only trying to calm her—but she didn't believe what he was saying. Paul's kidnapping showed how desperately he was bent on his course of action—there wasn't a chance in the world that she could reason with him. But she couldn't stand in front of the cabin arguing. She needed to get to Paul quickly, or it might be too late to save Sybil.

"I'll drive," Cos suggested.

Ari nodded.

She was glad to get in Cos's car and lean her head back against Cos's car seat.

"We've got to fatten you up," he said, glancing at her. "You look like you could use a good meal."

Ari smiled sadly and listened to the soft hum of the car's heater and the rumble of the tires

216

over the pavement. The headlights spotlighted wispy plumes of mist as they sped back toward town.

"How long have you known that Paul was guilty?" Cos asked.

Ari jumped. The word *guilty* had such an odd sound, as if Paul were human instead of a monster with evil and scarcely understandable appetites. She shrugged and looked away.

"Since he killed Susannah?" Cos suggested.

"Yes, I knew he killed Susannah," said Ari.

"Of course, Paul is your twin," Cos said. "Your instinct was to stick up for him. And I guess you hoped he wouldn't hurt anybody else."

"Yes." Ari gazed out the window. To Cos this was a simple case of a serial killer. He had no idea that she was up against an even greater evil. If he had known the truth about Paul, there was no way he would drive her to the apartment to "reason" with him.

"So that was why you left town so suddenly," Cos went on, his voice sounding reasonable. "It wasn't that you were afraid of the kids at school—you were afraid of Paul."

Ari shrugged. "Both."

Cos frowned. "Ari, why do you sound like you've given up? It's not over yet."

But for her it was. She only hoped that whatever Paul did to her didn't hurt more than she could bear. She couldn't even think past that point. "Cos—" she began. But the harsh sound of her voice frightened her, and she couldn't go on.

"What?" He watched her closely.

She licked her lips. "Listen. It's not possible to reason with Paul, because he's not . . . he's not all right. So when we get to his place, I'm going to go to him, the way he wants, and he's going to kill me, or anyway change me somehow so I won't be like myself—"

"Are you out of your mind?" interrupted Cos.

"Let me finish. I just want you to know before that happens—" she choked up "—that I love you."

"You *are* crazy," he said gently. "If you think I'm going to let you go in that apartment and put yourself at the mercy of a homicidal maniac, you've lost it. Pull yourself together." He glanced at her. "I guess I love you too. I've never worried about somebody so much in my life."

Ari smiled a little. "If you aren't going to let me go to Paul, then why are we driving back to town?"

"Because I hope that you can reason with him!" Cos shouted. "Because I'm an incurable optimist, and I keep thinking we're going to figure some way out of this mess. That's why!"

CHAPTER
NINETEEN

AS THEY APPROACHED THE ST. ANSELM'S CAMPUS, Ari saw that locating Paul's apartment would be no problem. It couldn't have been more conspicuous. Spotlights playing on the facade of an apartment building near the school focused on a fourth-floor window with a narrow balcony. She saw flashing blue police car lights and heard the strident electric sound of bullhorns, their message sounding garbled at this distance.

Suddenly she realized that a white-gloved officer loomed ahead of them. They had run into a police roadblock. The police were directing traffic away from the main road. Cos stopped and jumped out of the car. The cop strode toward him.

"I've got Paul Montclair's sister in the car," Cos explained. "She's come here to see if she can reason with him."

The officer spoke rapidly into a walkie-talkie, then gestured them on.

But instead of continuing on Massachusetts Avenue, Cos turned sharply onto the drive that went past the St. Anselm's tennis courts.

"What are you doing?" asked Ari.

"Cutting through campus."

"Can you?" She looked at him anxiously. "Does this road go all the way through?"

Cos frowned. "I hope so."

Ari saw the chapel rise on their right, a peaked roof among the trees. She felt disoriented. Suddenly the road narrowed, and she could see the end of it ahead in front of a loading dock behind the library.

"Damn," said Cos. He gunned the car, and it leapt the curb. They were going across grass then, and Ari clung to the armrest as they jolted ahead. A tree scraped the car. Then she spotted the low lights of the gym. She breathed a sigh of relief as their wheels bumped down once more onto a concrete drive.

Cos's face cleared. "We're okay now. That's the Activities Building."

"Stop!"

Cos suddenly jammed on the brakes.

A short distance ahead of them, through the bare branches of the trees, Ari could see searchlights and hear the electric crackle of police radios. Blue lights seemed to swim crazily in the mist.

She slipped from the car and stepped gin-

220

gerly over the corner of a playing field. As soon as she reached the Activities Building, she saw the shrub where she had left the chalice, and her breath quickened.

"What's going on?" panted Cos. He trotted up behind her.

Ari could see the faint glow of the gold. The shrub's dry branches scratched her hands as she reached for the chalice. The gold was cold and damp with dew. *If intensity of desire to talk is the secret, I should get Paul in loud and clear.*

Ari rubbed the chalice frantically against her jacket, and almost instantly Paul's image ballooned from it. She held it out before her. Paul's face was rounded as if she were looking at a hologram. His lips were parted expectantly. "Ari?" he said. "Is that you? Where are you?"

"Jeez, how does it *do* that?" whispered Cos.

Ari could feel Cos's warm breath on the back of her neck as he pressed closer to see, but she couldn't focus on him, or she might lose touch with Paul. "I'm very nearby," she said. "I'm across the street, behind the Activities Building."

Paul's face was radiant, and its bright glow cast long shadows in the night. The shadow of the shrub loomed as large as a scarecrow against the wall. "Come on up to the apartment!" Paul cried. "We can be together again."

Ari felt Cos's hands grip her upper arms tightly. "I can't," she whispered.

Paul's face grew dim. "You can't? Or you won't?" he said.

"Where's Sybil?" she asked him. She could feel the heat radiating from the chalice.

"Come up here and I'll tell you. You aren't going to find Sybil any other way—that's for sure."

"You haven't hurt her, have you?"

Paul's image faded and wavered. She repeated sharply, "Is she all right, Paul?"

"She's alive." Paul's mouth looked sullen.

"Did you hurt her?" Ari cried. "How could you do that?"

"I said she's alive," snapped Paul. "But I don't know for how much longer. You'd better hurry up, if you want to make sure she's going to make it."

"Paul, what's happened to you? How could you treat Sybil this way?" sobbed Ari.

"I need you!" Paul shouted. "I've got to have you! It's not wrong to take what you need! I'm through playing mind games, Ari. Get yourself over here, or I'm going to leave here without you and Sybil will die."

"You'll never get away! The place is surrounded."

He laughed. "They can't kill me, though, can they? In fact, they can't even touch me, because I've got a plan."

"What plan?" asked Ari quickly.

"That's for me to know and you to find out! Come on! If you come up here, you and Sophie

222

and me can all escape together. We'll be rich, Ari! And you and I can be closer than we ever were. Aren't you coming?"

"I don't know," said Ari. Suddenly Paul's image was as insubstantial as the mist at her feet, and then he was gone as if the image had never existed.

"How does that thing work?" whispered Cos.

"I don't know." Ari hugged it, unsure why she clung to it so desperately. What had it ever done for her? It had only showed her the vast gulf that had opened between her and her twin. She felt as if her mind were being split into two parts, each uncomprehending of the other. How could she go to Paul and let him make her into a vampire when he had become so alien and cruel? And yet how could she save herself and let Sybil die?

"We'd better let the cops know we're here," said Cos. "I don't want to be sneaking around over here in the bushes when some cop starts shooting." He guided her out to the street.

"You're holding me too tight," complained Ari.

"That's because I don't want to lose you." He landed a kiss on top of her head. "I wasn't exactly crazy about it when you said you weren't *sure* just now. What do you mean, you aren't sure? Your brother's out of his mind, Ari!"

Ari spotted Rab and Mr. Barron standing beside a police car and waved to them. Rab was a head taller than Mr. Barron, but as if in some instinctive sympathy, they stood in the same position, legs apart, hands clasped behind themselves. She and Cos made their way across the cables and wires that lay on the street and joined them on the sidewalk.

"You ought not to have come, Ari," said Rab. "The police are treating it like a hostage situation since they think there's a chance Sybil's in there. Right now he's sounding pretty desperate and anything could happen. Nobody's going to let you go to him. You could get hurt."

"But Sybil—" Ari began.

"It's very possible that Sybil is dead already," Rab said steadily. "It doesn't make sense for you to get killed too."

"Sybil's not dead," said Ari. "She's hurt, but Paul swore to me that he didn't kill her."

Rab passed his hand across his forehead. "You talked to him? How? The police have had the phone line tied up talking to him."

"She's got some weird walkie-talkie," put in Cos.

Ari realized she was no longer holding the chalice, and she looked around anxiously. "I must have dropped it or something. Did you notice what I did with it, Cos?"

Rab's eyes were drawn to the fourth-floor balcony where police searchlights crossed. His voice was anguished. "Where can he have put Sybil?"

Suddenly Ari was ashamed of giving any thought to the chalice. Cos was right—it was only a fancy walkie-talkie. It was worthless! All that mattered was getting Sybil out alive.

Mr. Barron's shoulders were stooped. "The police tell me that Paul told the mediator, in essence, to go to hell. He hung up. It doesn't look good."

"Ari's talked to Paul," said Rab suddenly. "He told her Sybil's hurt, but that she's alive."

"Hurt?" Mr. Barron gasped. "Did he say—"

Ari shook her head.

Suddenly a murmur went up from the crowd. Everyone was looking up, and Ari realized that Paul had stepped out on the narrow balcony. The balcony looked far too fragile to hold someone so big. He loomed high over its thin railing. The beams of the spotlights sank. "I bet they're trying to keep from blinding him with the spotlights so he doesn't fall," said Cos.

Ari was surprised at how massive Paul looked. She wondered if his immensity wasn't just some hallucinatory effect of her heightened consciousness and her fear. Their father had always seemed huge, too.

"Ari!" Paul screamed suddenly. "Where are you? I know you're out there!"

"What if he's got a gun?" said Cos. "Stay here, Ari."

But Ari jerked out of his grasp. "I'm Paul Montclair's sister," she told the officer standing by a spotlight.

"Here," he said, handing her a heavy flashlight. "Blink this so he sees where you are. We

225

don't think he's armed. If you want to stand out there on the sidewalk and talk to him, it ought to be okay."

Ari stepped onto the sidewalk, blinked the flashlight under her chin, and shouted Paul's name.

"Ari!" he shrieked. "You're down there! I can see you. Come on up!"

Ari had a sudden memory of a childhood vacation at a cold mountain lake. She had been standing alone on the bank. Paul had been drifting in a raft in the middle of the water; he had called for her to join him. He had always been the more daring of the twins, the first to try anything. *"The water's not so cold after you've been in awhile. You can do it. Come to me!"* She could hear his voice floating over the lake and over the years as clearly as a silver bell.

"I'm coming!" Ari called.

Paul whooped and threw his fist skyward.

But before she could move, Cos and Rab grabbed her arms. "You're not going anywhere, Ari," muttered Cos.

The night was raw, and the cold mist had settled on Ari's cheeks. She was mesmerized by Paul's beauty as she gazed silently up at him—that wild curly hair, the white shirt fluttering in the cold breeze, and the even whiter flesh underneath. He might have been the figurehead on a ship. Or a statue. In the stark light of the police spotlights, he looked as perfect and as unreal as a work of art.

"What am I going to do?" Ari twisted around, her eyes pleading with Cos. "I've got to help Sybil."

Then, as clearly as if it had been outlined in red marker, she saw the Jaguar parked at the curb. For some reason the car was rocking as if someone had jolted it. Its license plate said, "BLVDLVV."

"Blood love," said Ari aloud. What else could it mean? "That's got to be Paul's car!" she cried. "Look, it's rocking! I'll bet Sybil's in there!"

Rab released her and in a desperate sudden move grabbed the butt of a policeman's gun. Ari saw him jerk the gun free from its leather holster. Before she could even react, he was standing behind the black Jaguar, firing down at the lock of the trunk. She heard the shot explode and the sound of ricocheting metal. In the next instant the police fell on him, and the gun tumbled from his grasp into the gutter. Ari jerked the trunk open, her ears ringing with the noise of the gunshot and the smell of cordite stinging her nose. Its interior light showed the red flash of Sybil's hair. She was pale and breathing hard. A policeman bent at once and lifted her out.

When the gag was worked off her mouth, she coughed at first and couldn't speak. Cos produced a pocketknife and swiftly cut the brown nylon that held her ankles. Meanwhile a cop untied her wrists. Stunned, Mr. Barron stumbled over to her. Sybil threw her arms around his neck and sobbed. "My baby," he whispered, stroking her hair. "My baby."

Ari glanced up at the balcony then and saw that Paul was standing very still. He must have heard the gunshot. Perhaps through the mist he had seen his car's trunk fly open. Ari wondered if from his high perch Paul could see the golden gleam of Sybil's hair as, surrounded by her family and a gaggle of policemen, she was bundled up and lifted into a police car. His bargaining chip was gone.

"Ari," Paul yelled, "you saw that she was okay, didn't you? I'm not some monster. Come on up! I need you! I can't live without you—it's always been the two of us."

"I can't!" she screamed.

"You never loved me!" he yelled.

Suddenly he bent down and then disappeared into the black window. The curtains flapped loosely in the breeze.

Ari hugged herself and stared up at the empty balcony. She was cold. Beads of moisture were trapped in her hair, and her clothes were clammy.

Cos put his arm around her shoulders and squeezed. "Are you okay? Why don't I take you home so you can get some sleep?"

"Home?" She looked up at him blankly.

Cos looked momentarily staggered when it hit him that she had no home, but he recovered quickly. "I'm sure it'll be okay with my folks if you sleep at our place until you get something worked out."

"Just give me a minute." Ari pushed him away. "Honestly, I need to be alone."

He looked puzzled, but he stood back and let her walk away from him. The street was crawling with cops and police cars, so it seemed safe enough. Ari threaded her way through groups of police and mobile units, stepping over cables, until finally she spotted the telltale gleam of gold under a police car. She bent and retrieved the chalice, surprised to feel that it was still warm. Glancing around, she realized that everyone looked busy and preoccupied. Now that her part in the drama was over, she had become invisible to them.

She sat down on the curb between two police cars. "Paul?" She rubbed on the chalice hard. "Can you hear me?"

"Loud and clear." Paul's voice was dripping with sarcasm. "I guess you're heading off into the sunset with lover-boy, doing the happily-ever-after bit."

She could see her twin's face now, looking more real than when she had stared up at him on the balcony. "I love you, Paul. I just don't want to be a vampire. Can't you understand that?"

"Well, that's just not good enough, is it? Luckily, Sophie's with me all the way. She's at my side right now."

Paul's face was obscured by the glitter of

gold, and at first Ari thought she was losing the signal completely, but the quality of the glitter was odd—it shifted like vapor. Then she saw Paul's dark eyes peering at her, and she realized with a shock that he had put on a gold mask.

"What are you doing?" she cried.

"This is the plan, Ari." Paul's voice sounded muffled. "This is when the vampire gold does its stuff."

"What's the gold going to do?" asked Ari anxiously.

"Get us out of here," said Paul. "Sophie and I have been playing around with it, trying to see what it would do. Now you'll get to see, too. We're going to use it to get away."

"Don't!" cried Ari. "Paul, don't trust the gold! It's vampire gold."

He laughed shortly. "Well, Sophie and I are vampires. I guess you don't trust us any more than you trust the gold."

"But I do love you, Paul," Ari cried. Even as the words came out of her mouth, she wondered if they were true. Maybe she only loved the memories they shared.

She didn't even know if he had heard what she'd said. His image had vanished. She stared at the chalice a moment, then let it drop from her fingers. She heard a dull clang as it hit the curb and watched as it rolled into the gutter. She sat on the curb with her head in her hands until suddenly she heard a commotion behind her. She jumped up.

"Don't shoot!" someone shouted. "They're coming out."

The searchlights were beamed on the apartment's entrance. Ari realized that the police must be hoping to confuse Paul by shining bright light in his face as he came out. She had no idea whether that would work. There was a lot she didn't understand about her vampire twin's strange powers.

Suddenly she heard a sharp sizzle. She glanced down at the chalice lying in the gutter. Flames were licking at its jewels and sprouting from its rim. Ari stepped back sharply. It was a ball of fire no bigger than two fists. "Come out! Come out!" cried a shrill voice at her ear. Ari spun around, but no one stood behind her. The cold beam of floodlights played on the apartment entrance, and Ari felt a chill of fear. She wished she had stayed near Cos. She was sure something awful was going to happen.

"Stand back!" The police were shouting. "Stand back. They're coming out."

Ari's eyes were fixed on the glass door as it swung open, and she was instantly stunned by the dazzling brilliance of gold. The harsh light of the spotlights seemed to set it aflame. Paul and the girl were covered with gold! Their faces were hidden by thin gold masks, and somehow they had threaded gold disks together into belts and wrapped them around their bodies like chain mail. Jeweled gold plates were strapped to them in a kind of exotic plated armor. The effect was at once magnificent and barbaric, as if Paul and Sophie were tribal dancers stepping out of a dark jungle for the first time to astonish the modern world.

Ari saw that the walkway was lined with police, and she eyed them anxiously, wondering what they would do. She noticed that they were poised on the balls of their feet, with their hands hanging loosely at their sides, ready for action. Ari saw several of the officers glance at an older man, and it struck her that they must be waiting for his signal.

Paul and Sophie made their way between the lines of police, and Ari realized they were heading toward the black Jaguar. She caught the glitter of Paul's car keys in his hand. *And why shouldn't they drive away?* she thought, with a tiny flicker of hope. *They could make it.*

Suddenly she sensed movement. The line of police officers churned wildly and pressed toward Paul and Sophie. Paul and Sophie spun around. Two police officers in front lunged at them, then fell to the sidewalk as if they had struck an invisible wall. The officers sat frozen with astonished expressions on their faces as other officers leapt over them and clambered toward the gold-clad fugitives. In quick confusion they tripped, fell, and bumped into each other.

A murmur went up from the crowd, and Ari heard the sharp bark of Paul's laughter. The gold was protecting Paul after all!

Ari heard the explosive *whomp* of the Jaguar's

doors being slammed shut and saw the mellow gleam of the gold masks through the windshield. It looked to her as if now that Paul and Sophie were in the car, they were pulling off the masks. A cop tugged at the Jaguar's door handle, and Ari jumped as she saw him pull a gun. But before he could fire, the Jaguar's big motor rumbled. It sounded like a great beast coming out of hibernation. Suddenly it darted out into the road, its open truck bouncing wildly.

Ari heard the crackle of police radios and men shouting orders. Suddenly, in the midst of the confusion, Cos was at her side. They watched the Jaguar turn sharply, its lights illuminating the bare branches of trees by St. Anselm's back drive.

"He's turning onto the campus," Cos said.

Sharp voices filled the air and motors roared. Dark figures were running and shouting. Flashing blue lights bathed the sidewalk in an unreal glow.

An officer grabbed Cos's shoulder. "Son, where does that road he's taking go to? Do you know?"

Cos shrugged.

Ari shot a quick glance at him and squeezed his hand in gratitude. Maybe Paul would get away after all. The police didn't know the St. Anselm's campus. Maybe Paul was counting on that. A police car bumped up the drive behind him, but Paul was well ahead of him and driving fast. Ari saw the lights of the Jaguar flashing

233

past some trees in the distance. Then she lost it.

She and Cos exchanged a glance, and suddenly they were running. They both knew there were only two places where Paul could come out if he stuck to paved road. She and Cos cut across the playing field and ran past the refectory. Ari's breath was coming in painful gasps when at last she saw the tennis courts ahead. Paul would have to circle around the chapel, so there was a good chance she and Cos would get to the Massachusetts Avenue exit before him.

Cos grabbed Ari suddenly. "Hold up," he panted.

Then she saw the headlights beyond in the woods. Sirens rent the air, and blue lights flashed on the campus's stone buildings. "I don't think he's going to make it," she whispered.

She broke into a run and burst out onto the sidewalk that ran along Massachusetts Avenue. The broad street was empty except for a few scattered police cars. Ari sprinted down the sidewalk. She was desperate now for breath and had a painful stitch in her side. Suddenly the Jaguar shot out onto the avenue and skidded, its tires screaming. A resounding crash hit Ari's ears like a blow. The Jaguar had collided broadside with a police car. Shocked tears rose to Ari's eyes when she heard screams and an explosion. Flames leapt from the Jaguar's open trunk as if fire were its only cargo.

Ari could see police running toward the crash. "They're going to try to get them out,"

Cos said. "Maybe they'll be okay."

A chill seized Ari's heart as she watched. The curse of the vampire gold had lured Paul to his doom!

The Jaguar streamed flames like a meteor, and another explosion rocked the car. Its metal framework looked black in the flames. Ari saw police cars backing away from the blaze.

"Are you okay?" Cos asked anxiously.

Ari gulped and nodded.

Cos put his arm around her and held her tight. "Hang on," he said. "It's bad, but you know, maybe it's for the best with his legal problems and everything." Cos's face reddened self-consciously. He must have realized how insensitive that had sounded to her. "Did you say something?" He bent toward Ari anxiously.

She hadn't said anything, but a voice had sounded in her head, and it was almost as if he had heard it. Funny if Cos turned out to be psychic.

"It hurts," she said softly.

He kissed her. "I know, but I'm here. Hang on."

Ari knew she wanted to go on living. She belonged with Cos and Sybil. The small joys and small disappointments of life were all she wanted. But tears stung her eyes as she watched the terrible fire, burning with the fierce energy of a star, light up the night.

"Good-bye, Paul," she whispered. "Good-bye."

HAVE YOU READ?

VAMPIRE TWINS

A TRILOGY

BY JANICE HARRELL

1·BLOODLINES
2·BLOODLUST
3·BLOODCHOICE

AVAILABLE IN THREE
SEPARATE VOLUMES
OR A THREE-IN-ONE
EDITION